Modern Masquerade: Are You Brave Enough?

TORIA LEIGH

Published by Author Academy Elite
P.O. Box 43, Powell, OH 43035
www.AuthorAcademyElite.com

Paperback: ISBN 978-1-64085-311-9
Hardcover: ISBN 978-1-64085-312-6

Library of Congress Control Number: 2018943567

To the dreamers and the odd ones out,

To those who know there's more to life than fitting in,

May you always stay true to your identity.

IT WAS LIKE I WAS LIVING WITH A SPLIT
PERSONALITY. ONE SIDE OF ME WANTED NOT
TO CARE ABOUT WHAT PEOPLE THOUGHT,
BUT THE OTHER HALF WANTED NOTHING
MORE THAN TO BE LIKED.

Chapter 1

I didn't sign up for this. This was in no way, shape, or form my idea. In fact, I was entirely against it. But did anyone care? No. Parents overrule kids, so there I sat, headphones in, trying and failing to ignore my predicament.

Suddenly, I felt a tap on my left shoulder. Irritated, I removed my headphones and turned to my left where my dad sat. I responded to his tap. "Yes?" I saw Dad's giant smile.

When my dad is happy, you can see it shining through his eyes, which has always been one of my favorite things about him. When he's overjoyed, his eyes have a certain glow to them—this is one of those moments, I thought to myself. At the sight of my dad's glee, I instantly felt any irritation I had wash away.

"Are you excited about our vacation?" he asked.

I plastered on the best smile I could manage. "Oh yeah, I can't wait!" was my complete lie of a response.

My older brother, Darren, was sitting on my other side. Up until then, he had been distracted by a group of girls who had walked by. But of course, he decided this would be a good time to pipe in. "That's not what you've been—" I elbowed him before he could finish his sentence and ruin my dad's happiness.

Thankfully, my dad didn't hear what Darren started to say, because at the same time, the speaker sounded with the announcement, "Flight 422 to Chicago, Group C, please line up."

I muttered under my breath, "Saved by the speaker."

"What's that, sweetheart?" Dad asked.

I tried to cover up what I had said. "Oh, I was just wondering where Mom was?"

As if on cue, Mom came marching over with the confident sense of purpose she always had. *I wish I had that.*

"Guys, it's time to board. Someone wake up Ty." My mom was forever in command.

Darren and I looked at each other and in unison said, "Nose goes!" We each quickly put our fingers on our noses. Even my mom understood and did the same thing, but Dad just looked at us like we were crazy.

"What is the purpose of that? You all look ridiculous," he said. We all laughed.

"Dad, since you were the last one to get your finger to your nose, you lost. It looks like you get to wake Ty up. Have fun with that," I teased as I patted him on the shoulder.

Darren and Mom sauntered into line. I quickly placed my headphones back in my bag while Dad finished gathering his bag. I didn't want to wake Ty, because he was not exactly the most pleasant person when his sleep was interrupted. He tended to be mad for a while at whoever dared to jolt him from his slumber.

Dad was just about to rouse Ty, and I didn't want to be caught in the wake of Ty's wrath, so I walked over to Mom and Darren. "On the off chance there's a window seat available, can I have it?"

Darren shook his head at my request. "Nope, I'm older, so I would get it."

"That logic is flawed. I don't understand how age has anything to do with this."

At my answer, my mom sighed, already knowing where this was leading.

Despite my mom's reaction, I continued, "Besides, you may be older than I am, but we all know *I'm the more mature one*." I smirked and looked at Darren out of the corners of my eyes while he scoffed.

"Yeah, okay, you keep telling yourself that. I still get the window seat."

I was about to object when my mom cut me off. "Kinsley, it doesn't matter. There probably won't be a window seat available, so drop it. Besides, I'm not even sure we'll get seats together." I just huffed in response—*my mother, ever the problem solver, and me, ever the obedient daughter.*

"You know, we wouldn't even have to worry about getting seats together if we would fly a real airline and not a value one like Airstream," Darren said.

By now, Dad and Ty (who was not happy, to say the least) had made their way over to us.

"I don't believe you're the one paying for the flight," Dad responded to Darren.

We stood in line bickering over seating arrangements as Dad, being the peacekeeper, tried to figure how to upset the fewest people.

"If we're lucky enough to find an aisle with three seats available, how about Ty, Kinsley, and I sit together, and Mom and Darren try to find two open seats together?" my dad proposed.

I thought that was a fair arrangement, until Ty started complaining at this offer.

"No! I want to be with both you and Mom!" Even though Ty was nine, he whined so much, you'd think he was six.

Dad looked at me apologetically, and I answered before he could say anything. "I'm fine with that. I'll just sit with Darren." Dad gave me a look of gratitude, and I smiled back at him. I didn't mind. It meant I could listen to music on the flight and not be interrupted. *Plus,* I told myself, *Ty may be annoying, but I love him, so I would still do anything for him. Come to think of it, same with Darren.*

Once we started walking down the small aisle of the plane, Mom, Dad, and Ty went to the complete back of the plane in hopes of finding three spots together. I saw a row that had two free seats side-by-side and turned to point them out to Darren, but he wasn't behind me any longer.

Of course, Darren had already found a seat between two girls about his age who seemed to have no objection. They were already fawning over him, which was typical for him—at six feet, with dirty-blonde hair and Dad's inherited bright-blue eyes, he looked like a model and got attention from almost every girl he met.

I would be happy if I could even get attention from one guy. Apparently, I am sitting by myself, I realized as I daydreamed. I sat down in the aisle seat, thinking that if all the window spots were taken, I could at least stretch my legs into the aisle once we took off. I put my carry-on bag under the seat and got comfortable. I then remembered on the last flight I'd taken, I'd lost my watch at security. I grabbed my wrist and felt relieved when my fingers touched my cold bracelet.

To anyone else, it would seem like just a cheap old bracelet, but to me, it had significant value. It was a black leather bracelet with "A Princess Never Forgets Her Worth" engraved on a small metal plaque. My grandma had given it to me when I was younger. It's what gave my dad the idea to nickname me "princess"—which if you know me is ridiculous, because I am nothing like a princess.

I was knocked off my train of thought when I heard someone in the aisle ask if the seat beside me was taken. I looked up to reply and was surprised when I saw a boy, probably around my age, with light brown hair and blue eyes. His voice didn't match his appearance. It seemed too deep for his age. Something seemed familiar about him, but I was sure I hadn't met him before. *Maybe I saw him pass by in the airport.*

"No, go right ahead," I said as I stood up to let him in the row. He thanked me and sat down. Once he was situated, I sat back in my seat.

I leaned my head back against the headrest, since I was tired. I hoped to get some sleep, but the boy next to me apparently had other ideas.

"I'm Justin. You are?"

I turned my head toward him and politely answered. "I'm Kinsley."

I hoped he would drop the conversation at that, but apparently he wasn't finished. "That's a really cool name."

I smiled at his compliment. "Thanks." I hesitated before asking anything else. I wasn't really in a talking mood, and meeting new people wasn't exactly my favorite thing. They say people make up their opinion of others within the first few minutes of a conversation, and that idea terrified me. However, I knew the polite thing to do was at least to ask a question back. "What's bringing you to Chicago?" *That seems like a safe enough question,* I thought.

"I'm going to an event being held there. You?" Justin replied.

"That's cool, I'm just going on vacation," I said nonchalantly.

"That's cool." Before he could say anything else, the flight attendant interrupted with the speech about what to do if the plane were to crash and all that fun stuff. I leaned my head back and didn't really listen to what they were saying. Due to my parents' business and having family sprawled across the U.S., I'd flown so many times, I practically had the speech memorized.

It didn't take long for me to become caught up in my thoughts. *I'm not looking forward to this so-called vacation. It's not really a vacation at all. My family was asked to take part in a showcase for the arts, because my older brother is a singer, my younger brother is an actor, my dad works as a high-up business person in the arts industry, and my mom is a manager for people in the arts.*

Then you have me—that's it. I'm just me. I'm a normal, boring teen. I'm not in the arts industry, and I don't plan to be either. Mom and Dad have tried to persuade me to be anything from an actor to a dancer; they claim I'd be great, and I would love it. I think otherwise. However, I have thought about being a dancer. I dance in my spare time—but just for fun, to goof off. I'm not good enough to be a professional dancer.

I was pulled from my thoughts when I heard the engines get louder, and I realized we were taking off. I tried to lean forward a little to look out the window, which was kind of hard considering I was in the aisle seat. I'd finally just given up and leaned my head back, when once again the guy next to me started talking to me.

"Have you flown before?"

I inwardly groaned. *I swear he's doing it on purpose. Okay, that's ridiculous. He's probably just a talkative person. It's not that I don't like talking to people. I'm just tired and hoping to get some sleep.*

"Yeah, I've flown a lot. You?" If I wanted to sleep, I could just not ask him questions back; but I didn't want to come across as rude, and part of me enjoyed talking to him. It wasn't like I would ever see him again, so if I made a fool of myself, it wouldn't matter.

"Yeah, I've flown a lot as well. Have you ever been to Chicago before?" he asked.

"Yes, my grandparents used to live in Chicago, so I've been a lot. How about you?" He was about to respond, when over the speaker they announced that we could turn on electronic devices.

Once they finished speaking, he answered my question. "I've been once or twice, not a lot though."

I was debating whether I should ask him another question. One one hand, he'd been asking most of the questions, and I didn't want to be rude. But I also didn't want to end up talking to him for the entire flight.

Before I could decide, he spoke up again. "Well, I've talked your ear off long enough. I'll leave you alone."

I felt slightly bad after that. I didn't want to make him feel like he was a bother.

"No, it's fine, you're really not a bother." Which wasn't a total lie. He seemed pretty nice, and I enjoyed talking to him. Plus, I could always sleep at the hotel.

"Well, I'm glad I'm not annoying you." He didn't ask any more questions after that, and I didn't really know what else to say.

We sat in silence for a while. When I started to become worried about the silence growing awkward, I grabbed my headphones and iPhone out of my bag. Even with my music on, my thoughts spun a million miles an hour, diverting my attention from knowing what song was playing. I felt my eyes start to get heavy, and after a while, I was overcome by tiredness. Before I knew it, I'd fallen asleep with my head against the headrest.

Chapter 2

All of a sudden, I was roused from my sleep. I heard the voice over the speakers say to "put your trays in the upright and locked position and put away all large electronics." As I went to sit up, I realized my head no longer lay against the headrest. In fact, it was on another person's shoulder. I then remembered who was next to me, and I jolted up as quickly as I could.

"I'm sorry, I—" I started to apologize, but Justin cut me off.

"It's fine, don't worry about it." I could feel the heat rise to the surface of my cheeks, as I kept my eyes focused on the ground. I wished I could melt into the chair and disappear. I was embarrassed, to say the least. I tried to ignore my embarrassment as I wound my headphones up and shoved them back into my bag.

Surprisingly, Justin didn't say a word during our descent or when we taxied into the gate. Once the seatbelt sign went off, I grabbed my bag and waited until I could get out of the row. It wasn't until then that Justin spoke again.

"It was nice meeting you."

I turned around to face his voice and respond.

"You too." With that, I started to head off the plane.

Once I had exited, I found Darren waiting—leaning against a wall. I walked over to where he stood and waited for the rest of my family, since they had sat farther back in the plane. Ty, Mom, and Dad found us, and we all headed to baggage claim.

The whole walk there, Darren blabbed on about how great the flight was because he got to sit between two girls, and one fell asleep with her head on his shoulder. I felt heat creep up on my cheeks at the memory of my head ending up on Justin's shoulder, much like the girl next to Darren. I still felt badly for that, but as I could see from my brother's reaction, I was sure it didn't bother him that much.

We got to the baggage claim, and I walked over to the carousel where our suitcases were supposed to be. I waited until luggage started to come down the ramp onto the carousel. It didn't take long to find my luggage, because I had a customized suitcase. It was a black hardshell with a light blue silhouette of a dancer on it—and my name as well. I grabbed my bag off the carousel and wheeled it over to Ty and Mom, since they planned to watch the luggage while the rest of us retrieved the other bags.

We finished grabbing the rest of the bags, and we headed out the door to pick up our rental car. We had to take a shuttle to the rental car kiosk, since it wasn't on the airport's premises.

The shuttle ride was short and quiet, since we were all pretty tired—other than Ty who was fascinated looking at everything around him. As I looked at Ty, it was no shock that he was a child actor. He looked younger than he was—thanks to still having a baby face, which I guessed was good for acting. Also, I had to admit he was pretty cute. He had blonde hair, and he'd inherited mom's eyes; they were light brown with flecks of gold.

We pulled up to the rental car office and got our luggage off the shuttle. Dad went inside to talk to the people about the car, while the rest of us stood outside with the luggage and waited. I had gotten my headphones out and put one earbud in to listen to music. I saw Mom was trying to get Ty under control, since he was being super loud and energetic. She finally gave up and asked, "Can one of you please help and try and get him under control?" I looked over to see Darren too concentrated on his phone to notice that Mom had said anything. That, or he was ignoring her so he wouldn't have to help.

I took my earbud out and slid my headphones into my back pocket.

"Ty, how about we play a game?" I asked. He instantly went quiet with my question.

"What game?" he inquired, slightly tilting his head.

I thought for a moment. "What about the one-word game?"

His face lit up. Ty loved that game, even though it was super simple. All you did was say the first thing that came to your mind from the other person's word.

"Okay, sure! You start," he said nearly bouncing up and down.

I looked around, and the first thing to come to my mind was of course, "Car."

He thought for a while, then responded, "Taxi."

"New York."

"—City," he said.

I had to think for a minute, "Um…Los Angeles."

"Stars."

I was about to respond when Dad walked over with the keys to the rental car. "Alright let's go get our car," he said.

We followed my dad out into the lot of cars to the one we were renting. The rental car was a black SUV. We loaded our luggage and got inside. Our hotel was about an hour away, so I settled in to listen to music. *I'm shocked my battery is still lasting with how much I've been on my phone today.* I stared out the window at all the scenery passing by, and I soon drifted further into my thoughts.

I can't believe the rest of my family is all so excited about our so-called vacation—when in all reality it isn't a vacation at all. We're just going to some hotel for a showcase.

It was a showcase for the arts—like dancing, singing, acting, and modeling. My family was invited to be a part of the showcase. Not to be contestants, but to speak or teach classes, stuff like that. It was essentially a business trip. My thoughts drifted further.

I mean, on the other hand, I'm just along for the ride, since I'm not in the industry. I'm not important like the rest of my family. It must be nice to be wanted at an event—and to have fans. I guess it's a vacation for me, but if it goes the way I think, I'll be alone most of the time. That isn't bad for a little bit, but to be alone the whole time will be a bummer.

I wasn't sure how long I was off in my thoughts. Suddenly, one of my headphones was pulled out of my ear. I turned to see Ty was the culprit, but before I could respond and tell Ty how rude that was, he said, "Look! We're finally here." He pointed out the front windshield. My eyes followed his finger, and my jaw almost dropped. My parents may have said we were staying at a hotel, but calling it a resort was more accurate.

Let's just say this vacation may end up all right after all, I thought.

We pulled up in front of the hotel to put our stuff on a luggage cart. Once we had unloaded all the bags, Dad told us to wait in the lobby while he parked. Darren volunteered to go with him, so I pushed the cart into the lobby. I was instantly in awe. I marveled at the large lobby. It was gorgeous.

I quickly picked up that the hotel had a safari theme. In the center of the lobby was a big rock formation with a fake lion on top. Most of the flooring was hard and made to look like stone. However, part of the lobby had tan carpet with brown and green designs. As we entered, immediately to our right was a huge, wooden, dark-brown, check-in desk with gold accents. Out in front of the desk were a couple of brown leather couches and tan chairs. Plants appeared everywhere to tie-in the safari theme.

We sat on the leather couches to wait for Dad and Darren. As I marveled at the lobby, Mom asked, "So what do you think?"

Ty spoke up before I could even form an answer. "This place is so cool! I thought we were staying at a normal hotel, not a resort!" He was so excited, he nearly jumped out of his seat. I couldn't help but smile and slightly shake my head at his childish ways, but I couldn't blame him. I was as amazed at this place as he was.

"What about you, Kinsley?" Mom asked.

I smiled and responded honestly. "I like it. It's cool. The lobby is incredible."

She smiled victoriously. I loved to see my family smile—it was one of the best feelings in the world. I loved knowing that for a moment I was the reason for their happiness.

Just then Dad and Darren walked in. "I'm going to the front desk to get our room," Dad said.

Dad and Mom headed to the front desk, and Darren plopped down on the couch. Darren and Ty were talking about something I didn't have interest in, so I tuned them out.

I'd resumed looking around the lobby, when I saw a group of guys who seemed about my age walking toward one of the wings of the hotel, where I assumed the rooms were. The guys looked vaguely familiar to me, especially the tallest one, but I couldn't figure out why. I just waved the thought off. Dad and Mom returned from the front desk.

"OK, we got our room. Let's go find it," Dad said.

Ty walked ahead of us, Darren pushed the cart, and I traveled behind my parents. We went down the same wing the group of guys had just walked through. We entered an elevator and ascended to the third floor. When we stepped out of the elevator, I instantly noticed the green and tan carpet that matched the floor in the elevator.

A hall led to the left and right. Dad directed us to the right.

As we walked, I noticed decorative lights along the walls and overhead fluorescent lights. The hall was well-lit. We walked until we came to room number 308.

"Well, this is it. Are you guys excited?" Dad asked.

Before he could get the room key out of his wallet to let us in the room, Ty eagerly said, "Yes, so could you hurry up?!" Dad chuckled at Ty's enthusiasm and used the keycard to open the door.

It was a humungous hotel room—well, more like *rooms*. As we entered, to the right was a kitchenette with dark wood cabinets. Farther into the room, a family room welcomed us, the safari theme continuing. The family room was framed by orange and tan walls, with one wall displaying an orange, African safari mural. There was a dark brown, leather couch against the left wall and a TV across from it. Two chairs with black and white tribal print sat beside the couch.

I walked just past the kitchen. To the right, a door opened to a room with two queen-sized beds. I walked to the door-way on the other side of the family room, which led to a small hallway. I walked to the end of the tiny hall and found a room with a king-sized bed. I then checked out the other room on the right side of the hall; in that room was a single, queen-sized bed.

Just then, I heard Dad start to assign rooms. "Alright boys, you get the room with the two queen-sized beds; Kinsley, you get the room with the one queen-sized bed; and your mom and I get the king-sized bed." With that, I had to hug Dad. He was considerate enough to get me a room to myself.

"Thanks, Dad!"

"You're welcome. I figured you didn't want to share a room with the boys," Dad said.

Just then, Darren cut into the conversation. "Well, we see who Dad likes best. Why does Kinsley get a room all to herself? I'm the oldest!" I rolled my eyes at Darren's remark.

Before I could respond, Mom jumped in and saved the day, as always. "Darren, you know we don't pick favorites, and Kinsley only got a room to herself because she is the only girl. So quit complaining."

That shut down Darren's griping immediately. When Mom entered an argument, what she said next was law. I wished I had authority like that. Darren just huffed and didn't say another word.

"Okay, guys, we have an hour. Then the showcase director wants to talk with us to give us our schedules and discuss what we'll be doing," Mom said in her confident, no-one-gets-to-argue kind of way. My shoulders slumped, and my thoughts wandered.

Of course, the first day here, and everyone is already starting to work. I'm going to be forced to go to a boring meeting I'm not even a part of...lovely. If I had a penny for every time I had to attend a boring meeting I wasn't a part of, plaster a smile on my face, and pretend to be interested, I would be rich.

I walked towards my room. As I entered, I was amazed at how pretty it was. Centered against the left wall the bed sat with a dark-brown bedspread patterned with light-green accents. Tan carpet laid along the floor, and against the right wall sat a long dresser. I decided to start unpacking my clothes and put them in the drawers. I set my suitcase on my bed and began taking out my clothes.

Once I reached the bottom of my suitcase, I saw my masquerade mask. I had picked up my mask and started admiring all the intricate detail, when I heard the door to my room open. I felt my entire body tense as panic washed over me. Thankfully, my back was to the door, so I quickly dropped my mask back in my suitcase and turned around to see Mom standing in the doorway.

"Yes?" I said, acknowledging my mom's presence.

"Look, sweetheart, I know you're not thrilled about this vacation. So I wanted to make sure you knew that the showcase only goes for three days, and we're staying here a whole week. That way, we'll have some family time once the showcase ends, and you're more than welcome to hang around the showcase with us." Mom's voice remained soft.

"Cool, thanks for letting me know," was all I could think to say.

After that, she left the room. *Yes, I can be at the showcase— as long as I don't get in the way, is more like it. Why would I hang around a showcase where I can't contribute, and I would just be a burden more than anything? It's not like anyone wants me there. I think I'll pass.*

I sighed and turned back around. I looked at my mask lying in the bottom of the suitcase, and I couldn't help but pick it up again. The black, blue, and silver stared back at me. As if in some trance, I slowly put the mask on my face. I pulled the black strap over my head and gazed in the mirror. The mask would be the shape of a crescent moon if not for the ring around my right eye–which extended beyond the crescent. The mask covered the entire left side of my face— and my lips, chin, and nose. The right side of the mask came to a point at my lower jawline, covering the lower part of my cheek. The mask also circled my right eye. All that remained of me was my eyes, a sliver of skin on my right cheek, and a glimpse of skin on the right side of my forehead.

I shook myself out of my trance and took off my mask, grabbed my messenger bag from the floor, and emptied its contents. I then filled it with a pair of black exercise capri pants with a blue stripe that started at the hip and went all the way down to the ankle, a blue tank top with the words "she believed she could so she did" across the chest, my portable speaker, my camera, and last but not least, my mask. It all fit perfectly in the bag.

If someone happened to see the contents of my bag, I'm sure they would be confused. A mask was not exactly the typical thing a 14-year-old girl would be lugging around.

I grabbed my iPhone and headphones, shoved them into my pockets, and went out to the family room. I entered to find Ty, lounging on the couch, texting a friend. Yes, he was nine, but he had more friends and a better social life than I had, go figure.

I sat down on the couch next to him, and he glanced over at me. "So do you like your room?" That question made him smile.

"Yeah, it's awesome!" he said.

I smiled, loving his enthusiasm. "Are you excited to help out with the showcase?" I asked.

He nodded his head and gave no more of a response, because he was too consumed with texting to give a real answer back.

I decided to turn on the TV, since texting currently out-ranked me. I flipped through the channels until I found something I was even remotely interested in watching. That kept me occupied until Mom and Dad came out of their room and told us to get our shoes on. I turned off the TV, quickly slipped on my shoes, and grabbed my bag. *Let the "fun" times begin…*

Chapter 3

Dad led us to a different wing of the hotel with the ball-rooms and convention rooms. This hall dead-ended into a split that went left or right. Dad went left. We all followed him, since we had no idea where we were going.

This hall felt more business-like than the rest of the hotel. The safari theme still showed, but it was much more understated.

The activity around us took me by surprise once we turned the corner. It went from being deserted to having crew members zipping to and from the area like in a hive of bees. The only thing going on that day was setup, so we saw only crew members and speakers—no contestants.

We stopped at a table being set up. I assumed it was where all the contestants would check in for the showcase.

Dad spoke to the people at the table. "We're the Radfords."

One of the people setting up the table finally noticed us and looked up from what she was doing to respond to my dad's introduction,. "Oh! Hello, I'm Rachel, the head director of the showcase." Mom and Dad shook her hand and introduced themselves,—then Ty, Darren, and me. I just smiled politely and shook her hand. "If you guys would follow me, I will take you to a conference room and we can get everything sorted out," she said in a polite but all-business kind of way.

She took us to the end of the hall. "Right in here, and I'll be with you in just a minute." In the center was a huge conference table where we all took seats. I snagged a seat closest to the door.

Everyone was quiet, until I spoke up. "Mom, I don't understand why I have to be here. I'm not contributing to the showcase in any way, shape, or form."

She was just about to reply when Rachel entered the room. "All right, let's get started. We will begin with what is going on each day." We all nodded in response to signal to her we were paying attention. "Today is set-up. Tomorrow is singing and modeling. The next day is dance and acting. Then the last day is a masquerade ball for the contestants and their families along with the agents, managers, and casting directors." My parents and brothers vocalized their understanding with various "okays" and "cools."

I merely nodded, not feeling the need to speak.

Rachel continued. "All right, now we need to discuss what parts we want you to attend, when you will be speaking, and in what rooms." I took that as my chance to sneak out, since she had gotten out a full-blown schedule of the showcase and handed it to everyone but me—since I wouldn't be doing anything.

No one was paying attention to me anyway. I'm sure I could get in trouble later for sneaking out of the meeting, but I really didn't care.

It's not like it even matters, I told myself. *It was pretty much like I didn't exist. I don't matter regarding the showcase. Therefore I'm sure it doesn't matter that I miss the meeting. I mean, it's not like it would have been the first meeting I sat through that didn't involve me. Skipping one won't hurt, right?*

I normally wouldn't care if I had to sit through a meeting. I'd just do it without complaining. However, after a long plane flight, I wanted nothing more than to stretch my legs. I decided to explore the event area.

I walked down the hallway, which by that time only had one or two workers. All the hustle and bustle had died down—I guessed because they'd finished setting up everything. I looked in a room that I assumed housed the main part of the expo, due to its big stage and many chairs not yet fully in place. People were still setting up chairs and talking about the lights and such.

I watched as a man barked orders at workers. I presumed he was the man in charge. It wasn't long before he noticed me and eyed me wearily. I took that as my cue to leave. Since I was not part of the setup crew, I was afraid I would get in trouble for being somewhere I wasn't allowed.

I decided to walk down the other side of the hall where it had split. It seemed deserted. I peeked in one of the rooms and saw it had a stage that was similar to the one for the showcase. *That's weird. I thought the entire showcase would only have one stage.*

The room was empty, so I figured it was done being set up. I walked farther inside and let the door shut behind me. I walked up to the stage and considered hopping up on it, but then I thought I heard one of the doors shut in the back of the room. I looked and didn't see anyone. I mentally debated whether I should get up on the stage or not. I finally decided against it, in case someone would come in and get me in trouble. My parents would be furious at me if that happened.

I walked through the door to the main hall and headed in the opposite direction of my parents. At the end of the hall, it turned left. I followed it to another corridor of rooms. I peeked into a room and saw it was a smaller room with nothing set up in it. Since everything in this wing looked like it had already been prepared, I assumed this room wasn't in use—but I wanted to make sure.

I closed the door and just happened to see a woman in a hotel uniform walking by. "Um excuse me, this room isn't going to be in use, correct?" I asked.

She glanced down at her clipboard and responded, "It doesn't look like it."

I smiled. "OK, thanks." She nodded and walked off.

I remembered passing a women's bathroom, so I walked back down the hall. I entered the bathroom, went into the largest stall, unzipped my bag, quickly threw on my exercise clothes, and exited the bathroom.

I took a moment to check the hall for any other people before I entered the room. Upon entering, I noticed the room had brown carpet and tan walls. The only furniture was chairs stacked along the wall opposite the doors. I opened my bag and removed my camera and portable speaker. I paired my phone with my speaker and set up my camera. Once everything was ready, I unzipped my bag and pulled out the last piece of the puzzle—my mask.

Chapter 4

I looked at my mask in my hands for a minute, as it stared back at me. I ran my hand along the royal blue and silver designs on the front. It felt almost like holding a piece of myself.

I pulled myself out of the trance. I took a moment to glance around the room and listen for any voices in the hall. Once I was confident the coast was clear, I pulled on my mask. Such a familiar feel, it almost brought me comfort.

I set my camera to the filming setting. I hesitated before hitting the button. It didn't matter how many times I made these videos, I still got nervous. The added pressure that someone could walk in at any minute didn't help. However, I knew I would be quick enough that no one should find out. I took a deep breath and hit record. It didn't matter if the video showed me coming back from pressing the button or if there was a pause at the beginning; I would just edit it out later.

I stood in front of the camera and talked as if I were addressing an audience. "Hi everyone, I am Incognito Moves, as some of you may know. But if this is your first time watching, then welcome. For those of you who don't know about me, I'm a dancer, and I always wear my mask to protect my identity. Enough about me, let's get to dancing. This song was a request from a fan. I hope you enjoy it." With that, I pressed play on my speaker and moved into position before the song started.

The music began, and my body awakened. Commanded by the music, my arm was the first thing to move in rhythm with the music. The motion slowly flowed from one arm to the other and then cascaded down to my feet. As the song continued, I transitioned between fast and precise to elegant and graceful as my movements followed the ebb and flow of the music.

My moves were freestyle, since I hadn't choreographed an actual dance to this song before, but that was the way I liked it. I made up everything as I went along. Each move was spontaneous, directed by the song. No planned steps, no worries. As I danced to the rhythm of the song, I quickly lost myself in the music and motion.

When I was moving, none of my problems existed. I released all of my pent-up emotions as I danced, using all of my heart and very little of my head. I let my anger and irritation at the showcase fuel the intensity of the dance. As I moved about the room, it was like wringing out a towel. All of my hurt from being invisible dripped into the dance. I was, piece by piece, being woven into the dance. The more I danced, the more I released, and the freer I felt. As I fell farther under the spell of the music, I lost my need for perfection. I lost myself and found myself all at the same time.

Once the music finished, I walked up to the camera, feeling raw and out of breath, and said, "I hope you enjoyed the video. Feel free to leave any other suggestions for songs in the comments. You never know, it may be the next song I pick. Incognito Moves, signing off." Just as I turned the camera off and was about to return it to my bag, I heard clapping coming from the doorway.

Startled, I whipped around to see who the person was. Before me stood a boy, who appeared to be 16. He had short, light brown hair. My attention instantly drew to his striking light-blue eyes. Shock shuttered through me when I realized it was none other than the guy from the plane. My fear froze me. I didn't know how to react. *Was he stalking me? Did he see me without my mask? Did he recognize me? Should I run—or ask him something?* All these questions were sprinting through my brain at a million miles an hour.

He interrupted my thoughts. "That was amazing!" I had no clue what he knew or what he wanted. My body stood on edge. Every muscle was tense waiting for what would happen next.

My voice was weak when I mumbled, "Uh, thanks…" I paused, waiting to see if he'd respond, and decided I should start packing up my stuff as quickly as I could. The guy took another step into the room, not noticing my apprehension toward him—*or not caring*.

It was then that he decided to say something again. "You know, I've always wanted to see Incognito Moves dance live. Don't get me wrong, the videos are great, but they don't do your dancing justice."

I was still jamming stuff into my bag, trying to avoid look-ing at him as much as possible without being rude, and not succeeding in that aspect. "Really?" was all I said in response. I didn't know what else to say! Once I was done packing up everything but my mask, which was the only thing still pro-tecting my identity, I was forced to turn around to face him.

"Yeah, I've watched nearly every one of your videos," he said. It was only a beat before he continued, "Sorry, that sounds like I'm an obsessed super fan. I just think you're a talented dancer." I couldn't help but crack a small smile under my mask. Unlike with my brothers, it wasn't every day that I got to meet a fan in person.

I relaxed slightly, figuring he wasn't here to kidnap me. My shoulders released ever so slightly, and I noticed the sweat that had formed in my hands. He hadn't seen me without my mask, and while so captivated in meeting a popular YouTuber, he had no idea who I was. It was in that moment that it dawned on me who was standing in front of me. When I saw him on the plane, I had thought he looked familiar but couldn't figure out how I knew him.

"Thanks. It's not every day I get to meet my fans. I'm surprised someone from Advanced Company even knows I exist," I said.

A wide smile grew on his face at my response, despite the fact that he was obviously surprised I knew who he was. *I can't believe I didn't notice who he was on the plane. He's only in one of the most up-and-coming dance groups.*

"You know who I am?" he asked, surprise evident on his face.

"Yes, I do, you're Justin from Advanced Company, the best up-and-coming dance group. I must confess, I've also watched all of your group's videos. You guys are great," I said, unable to maintain eye contact but still hoping he could hear the sincerity in my voice.

"Thanks! I'm not sure I would say we are the best up-and-coming, but we're certainly starting to catch some recognition." He paused slightly before continuing, "It's cool to know that Incognito Moves watches our videos."

I began fiddling with my hands. "I think it's more the other way around; you guys are the ones who are basically famous."

It dawned on me how long I had been talking to him, and I was afraid that after the initial hype of meeting me wore off, he would recognize me as the girl on the plane. I made a beeline for the door. Since he stood in my way, I had to go around him.

"It was nice getting to meet you, Justin, but I must be going." I talked as quickly as I was walking. I maneuvered around a slightly confused Justin and flew out the door.

I quickly returned to the ladies' bathroom where I initially had changed. I entered the bathroom before he could realize where I had disappeared to. I gingerly removed my mask and changed back into my normal clothes, stashing my dance outfit in my bag. I waited in the bathroom for a while, just to be safe and make sure he was gone, before embarking down the hall toward the conference room where my family initially was.

Hopefully they're done with their meeting now, and I can apologize for leaving. Hopefully my parents aren't too upset with me.

I pulled out my phone to make sure I hadn't missed a text message or call from my parents. Suddenly, I smashed into someone else, and my phone dropped out of my hand. I was able to regain my balance and keep from falling over completely. I bent down to pick up my phone, and I quickly uttered, "I'm so sorry."

"It's totally fine. I wasn't watching where I was going, so I'm also guilty," the guy assured.

Oh no, I know that voice. It can't be him. I looked at him for the first time since colliding, and of course, it just had to be Justin. *Really, what are the chances?*

"Wait a minute," he said as he eyed me curiously.

I held my breath. *Oh no, he knows who I am. He's put the pieces together.*

He continued, "You're the girl I met on the plane… Kinsley, wasn't it?" I let out a breath as I felt my body un-tense. He didn't have a clue.

"Yep, that's me. You're Justin, right?" I replied.

"The one and only," he said with a smile, his arms slightly extended out as though to say, *here I am.*

I smiled in response to his quip. I figured the polite thing to do would be to ask him something to keep the conversation going. "So what's the reason you're here? Vacation?" I asked.

"No, I'm here for a show. I'm in a dance group called Advanced Company," he said, blowing it off like it was nothing.

"Oh, I think I've heard something about you guys; that's cool." Well, that wasn't a lie exactly; it just wasn't the full truth.

"Are you here for vacation?" he asked.

I quickly searched for the right words. "Well, sort of… it's a long story," was the best thing I could come up with to keep the conversation short or at least moving in a different direction.

Hopefully, you won't ask what that long story is.

"I've got time," he said with a smile.

Of course you do. That was not the answer I was hoping for or expecting. I should have ended the conversation by now, and then I wouldn't have to explain that I am the lame one in my family.

I searched for the best way to explain my situation without sharing too much—or so little that he would ask more questions.

"My family was invited to help and be part of a showcase for the arts. My parents still want it to be a vacation, so I guess you could say it's both business and vacation… OK, I guess it's not that long of a story." I laughed at my awkwardness.

He chuckled at my joke. "Your family's participating in a showcase. That most likely means someone in your family is a performer. Is it you?" He seemed genuinely interested.

I quickly shook my head no and was quick to counter his thought. "No, I have two brothers. One is a singer, and the other is an actor. My dad is also doing stuff on the business side of it, and my mom is a manager, so that's why we're here."

"Wow, your whole family is in the arts industry. What about you?" he asked.

Are you ever satisfied? Do you ever stop asking questions? It doesn't matter what I do. Why do you care?

When I realized I was fiddling with my bracelet, I shoved my hands in my pockets to stop from fidgeting.

"No way, performing is not for me. I like the arts, and I'm a fan of dance—but I don't partake in the arts. Guess I wasn't gifted that way." Well, that wasn't a total lie. I didn't partake in the arts *as myself.*

Justin nodded, taking in my response, when all of a sudden I could tell something popped into his head. "Hey, you said you were a fan of dance. You should meet the rest of my group."

"Oh, no, I'm okay. I wouldn't want to bother them or intrude." I hoped to get Justin to drop the offer. *Yeah, it would be cool to meet the group, but I don't want to be asked any more questions. Besides, I'm sure I would just get in the way.*

"No, it's the least I could do for nearly knocking you over like the dork I am," he said persuasively.

I was trying to figure out if he was genuinely kind—or had some other motive. I thought for a moment about his offer. *It's not like my family even cares where I am at the moment, and it would be cool to meet them, so why not? I won't stay long. I'll just meet everyone, then leave.*

"Sure, if you're certain I wouldn't be intruding, I would love to meet them."

Justin smiled victoriously at my answer. "Right this way." He led me around the corner and past the room where I—I mean, Incognito Moves—had danced.

"So are there other performers in the show, or just you guys?" I think my question shook him out of his thoughts, because it took him a minute to realize what I was asking.

"What? Oh, yeah no. We aren't the only ones. There are others. We aren't popular enough to be headliners yet."

"Makes sense," was all I said.

Thankfully, before Justin could ask me a question, he stopped in front of a door, opened it strategically, and motioned to the doorway.

"Ladies first!"

I smiled. "Thank you." *Wow, I can't believe there are still gentlemen these days,* I thought as I stepped into the room.

Chapter 5

Once through the door, I saw three other guys who I recognized as the rest of Advanced Company. As soon as I entered the room, all the guys' heads snapped in my direction. I could tell they were a little surprised to see me. They were probably expecting only Justin.

Justin apparently didn't feel the need to explain how he had met me. Instead, he instantly started introducing me to the other members.

Justin pointed to the shortest one of them, and if I had to guess, the youngest. He appeared to be 13. He had a very young face with boyish features. He had tanned skin, light-brown hair, and chocolate-brown eyes that seemed to shine with curiosity.

"This is Tommy." Tommy waved when he was introduced.

Justin moved on to the only blonde of the group, who was about my height and seemed to be 15. He had light-blue eyes and fair skin. He was thinner than the other guys in the group and seemed to have spindly arms and legs, despite not being very tall.

"This is Adam." Adam smiled and gave a nod when introduced.

Justin then gestured to the last guy left. He was taller than Adam, but maybe just slightly shorter than Justin. *He's probably Justin's age,* I thought. He had black, spiked hair and amber eyes that seemed to scream mischief.

"Last but not least, this is Nick." Nick winked at me when introduced. I wasn't sure if I should be flattered or upset.

Justin explained Nicks behavior. "Just ignore him. He does that to almost any girl he meets." When I glanced back at Nick, there wasn't any sign that he was irritated by Justin's comment.

I guess he doesn't care. I nodded and made a mental note to remember that Nick was just a flirty person.

"Are you here to see the show?" Nick asked with a confident smile.

I assumed he thought I was some fangirl who ran into Justin and wanted to meet the rest of the group, so he wanted to come across as charming.

"No," I said with emphasis, "My family is here for a showcase."

"Are you a performer?" Tommy asked, his eyes wide with excitement.

I shook my head and responded with a simple no. I didn't feel the need to explain the whole "only one not in the industry" thing.

"Well, now you can say you've met Advanced Company. Not that that is a very exciting thing," Justin said.

I smiled warmly before responding. "You guys seem pretty cool, so it seems like a win to me. To be honest, I usually don't like meeting famous people, because I'm always afraid they'll be stuck up—or mean." *Why did I say that? There was no reason I should have responded like that. They didn't need to know that. I'm such an idiot. Why can't I just keep my mouth shut?*

Tommy quickly spoke up. "I don't think we're mean or stuck up; but then again, maybe I'm wrong."

I released a tiny lighthearted laugh; he reminded me a little bit of my younger brother, even though Tommy wasn't as young as Ty. "From what I've seen, you guys seem pretty nice."

Tommy smiled widely after my reassuring statement.

"You said you don't like to meet famous people. You're implying you get the opportunity to meet stars quite frequently?" Justin asked curiously.

I looked down at the floor. *If I answer Justin's question honestly, they're going to think I'm weird or it's going to start a disagreement. However, I don't want to lie either.*

I knew I had to answer his question truthfully, but I was already regretting what I was about to say. "Yes. Due to my mom and dad's work, I get the chance to meet some famous people on occasion. However, I don't see it as anything special. They're just normal people like you and me."

Nick laughed. "Yeah, special people who have awesome jobs, are rich, and known by many thousands of people."

I knew I would get a response like that. I always do. I searched for the best way to get my point across. Then it hit me.

"You guys are dancers. You tell me: what's the difference between you and a famous dancer?" I asked.

Nick was about to speak, but Justin purposely cut him off. "Nothing, other than the famous dancer has commonly been dancing longer and is known by more people—but is still just an average person with skill."

I smiled at Justin as a way to give him a silent thanks for stopping Nick from talking. I fiddled with my hands, not knowing what to do or say next. I noticed Nick eyeing my bag.

"I like your bag. It's cool."

"Thanks, my dad got it for me a while ago." I tried to shift my bag a little further behind me. I was worried Justin would notice it as the same one that Incognito was carrying.

It was not exactly a discrete, common bag. It was black with distinct, bright blue designs.

Just then, my phone vibrated in my pocket, and I took it out to see that my dad was calling me. I suddenly remembered I had snuck out of the meeting and hadn't checked in since then. A slight wave of panic went over me. "I'm sorry, I have to answer this."

They all responded with things along the lines of "no problem" or "no worries."

I answered the phone and slowly stepped away. The boys instantly fell into an effortless conversation, so I didn't have to worry about them listening in.

"Hello," I answered.

"Hey Kins." I heard Dad's voice as he began to speak. "We were wondering where you are. We're back at the hotel room, and we want you to come back up."

"I'll be right there; just give me a few minutes," I said.

"Okay, I'll see you in a few," Dad said.

"Okay, bye."

I hate when Dad calls instead of Mom. It's impossible to tell over the phone if Dad is upset or not. However, with Mom, I know right away. I turned back to Advanced Company.

"I'm sorry, guys. That was my dad. I have to go. It was nice to meet you all." They all said bye and that it was nice to meet me. "Well, hopefully I'll see you guys around." I waved and walked out of the room.

I sighed once I had exited, and I began my trek back to our room. My thoughts wandered...

They all seem nice. Tommy is just adorable. He still has that little kid kind of cuteness. Adam appears to be a tad shy, but I'm sure once you get to know him he'd be more talkative. Nick, on the other hand, seems very outgoing and like the troublemaker of the group. Justin, he's a mix; he's more outgoing than Adam, but I also see how he's more reserved than Nick.

On the one hand, it was cool that I got to meet Advanced Company, but on the other hand I kind of hope I don't run into them again. I'm worried that the more time I spend around Justin, he'll put the pieces together and figure out I'm Incognito. Then he'll tell the guys, and my secret will be out.

My fans have been asking who I am—and for me to reveal myself. One post about my identity, and there goes any privacy I wanted. I'm not famous enough for my whole life to change just from unmasking myself, but I'm not ready for people to know who I am—at least not yet. It is a really big hotel. I shouldn't run into them that much, and if I do, it's not like they probably would do more than acknowledge me and be on their way again. I'm sure everything will be fine.

I reached our hotel room and suddenly remembered everything was not fine. I could be facing two very disappointed parents on the other side of the door. I stood staring at the door for a few seconds. I took a deep breath, mentally preparing myself for whatever was on the other side, and I opened the door.

"I'm back," I announced as I entered. I was surprised to find everyone in the family room. I figured the boys would be in their room or out doing something.

Mom and Dad seemed to be in the middle of a conversation, Darren was listening to music, and Ty was watching TV. Mom and Dad were the only ones to become aware of my presence.

"Did you have fun?" Dad questioned.

I just nodded my head with a simple "yeah," waiting for the next part to come.

When Mom responded with a cheerful, "That's great!" I just stood, baffled.

I finally got my wits about me and decided to ask the dreaded question: "Wait, I'm not in trouble for sneaking out of the meeting?"

I heard my dad give a small stifled chuckle as though that were a crazy thought.

"No, we knew a meeting you didn't have to be a part of would be boring. It honestly just came as a surprise to us. We would expect something like that from Darren, but not you," Mom said with a light tone.

"Oh," was all I could manage.

I guess they don't see it as a big deal. It was only surprising behavior from me, because I try and be the best daughter I can. I think about doing stuff like that all the time, but I refrain, because I want to be a good daughter. I have to bring something to the table, since I'm no benefit in the performing category like the boys. I guess this just proves my initial thought that they don't care where I was. Don't get me wrong, I'm happy I'm not in trouble; but just once it would be nice to know someone wanted me around.

My growling stomach brought me out of my thoughts.

"What are we doing for dinner? I'm hungry," I asked.

By then, Darren had taken his headphones out. "We decided on pizza."

"Sounds good. Tell me once it gets here; I'll be in my room." I walked off to my room and closed my door. I dropped my bag at the foot of my bed and grabbed my laptop from the side table, removing my camera from my bag.

I sat down on my bed, took the memory card out of the camera, and downloaded the footage from earlier that day to my computer. Once it was downloaded, I did some minimal editing and posted it to my YouTube account—or should I say, Incognito Moves' account?

Once it was uploaded, I shut down my computer and set it on the table in the corner of the room. I put my camera back in my bag and set my bag in the corner of the room under the table. I got out my iPhone and headphones and sat back down on my bed. I started to listen to music and look at Twitter.

At that time, I was on my personal account, not Incognito's. I went to Advanced Company's Twitter page to see the latest tweet and couldn't help but smile a little. The tweet read, "So happy. You'll never guess who I ran into: Incognito Moves. It turns out she's a fan of us!" Under the tweet was Justin's name, showing he was the one who had posted.

I switched to Incognito's account, went back to that tweet, favorited it, and retweeted it. I retweeted some fans who had tweeted me, and then I heard a knock on my door. I pulled my headphones out and said, "Come in."

The door opened to reveal Darren. "Pizza's here," was all he said.

He walked away just as I was responding with, "All right." I logged off Twitter and went into the family room to eat with everyone.

Once everyone was finished eating, since it had been a long day of traveling and everyone had an early wake-up the next morning, we decided going to bed would be best. *Well, me waking up early tomorrow is optional,* I figured, *but why waste the whole day sleeping?* I withdrew to my room and threw on my fuzzy pajamas, quickly brushed my teeth, and washed my face. *I'm not sure why I bother with washing my face when I still get acne anyhow. I guess I'm not one of those lucky girls who have a perfect complexion and flawless skin; wouldn't that be nice?*

I set my alarm clock, pulled back the covers, and slid into bed. Despite my efforts to fall asleep, I remained wired. I looked at the inscription on my bracelet: A princess never forgets her worth.

That requires having worth in the first place, I thought, drifting off to sleep.

Chapter 6

I woke to my alarm clock blaring in my ear and nearly giving me a heart attack. I leaned over and fumbled with my alarm clock a few seconds until it finally stopped. I flopped back over and laid in bed for a few more minutes, wondering if anyone else in my family was up yet. When I couldn't procrastinate any longer, I dragged myself out of bed and got ready for the day.

Once I was dressed, I went on a search for my family, hoping that I could still have breakfast with them. I reached the family room, but nobody was there. I stood still for a minute, listening for any squeak of sound—nothing.

I walked down the hall and peeked into my parents' room, only to confirm my suspicions that no one was there. *Well, I might as well check the boys' room, even though I'm pretty sure they're already gone.* I went back down the hall and crossed the family room again to the boys' door. I pulled the door ajar far enough to see that they were gone. *Go figure.*

I sighed and turned back to face the family room. I stood staring at the empty chairs and realized I was going to be spending most of the day by myself.

Not that this is any different than on a normal basis.

I ignored the gaping silence, returned to my room, snatched my headphones and iPhone, and headed toward the door. I stopped dead in my tracks when I saw a sticky note on the inside of the front door in my mom's handwriting. I peeled it off and read it out loud: "Sorry we had to leave so early and miss breakfast, Kins. We love you. Darren performs today, and we want you to be there to support him. The singing part starts at 4:30. Don't be late."

I released a heavy sigh. *Of course, the one thing they're concerned about is me making Darren's performance, not what am I going to do the entire day by myself. So much for "family vacation."*

I crumpled up the note and threw it in the trash. I pulled out my phone and glanced at the time. It was only 8 a.m., so I had a LOT of time to kill until Darren performed. I made my way to the elevator with my mind on Darren's singing act.

He won't notice if I'm there or not. I'm not sure why Mom and Dad care so much.

I made it to the elevator and pressed the button, waiting for it to come. I realized how pathetic I sounded. I argued with myself.

I should be there to support Darren. If I had a performance of any kind, he would be there for me. It's what siblings do.

The ding of the elevator arriving brought me back to reality. In the brief seconds before the doors opened, I kept thinking, *please don't be anyone in there, please don't be anyone in there. I am in no mood to talk to people.* The doors soon slid open only to reveal one lone person. I inwardly groaned, *this just isn't my day.*

It was none other than Justin. As I stepped inside, he looked up from his phone. I saw realization flash across his face, and I watched a small smile appear.

"Fancy seeing you here," he greeted me.

I flashed a brief smile but didn't say a word.

I guess he took my smile as an invitation to start a conversation. "Where are you headed?"

I thought, *does it matter?*

"I'm going to breakfast. You?" I did my best to make my tone cheery.

"Same. The boys are already down there waiting for me."

"Nice," I said while keeping my sights locked on the panel of buttons. *Really, "nice" is the best I could do?* I found myself at a loss for words. I mentally cursed myself for being bad at interacting with strangers. I felt my fingers start to mess with my bracelet. The quietness made me uncomfortable.

"You eating by yourself, or is someone waiting for you?" He filled the awkward silence.

I swear, talking to this boy is like playing 20 questions. "By myself. The rest of my family has already eaten breakfast," I said nonchalantly, in hopes he wouldn't make a big deal of me eating alone.

Without hesitation he offered, "Why don't you eat with us? I'm sure the guys wouldn't mind."

From any other person, his offer would have caught me off guard. But from him, I half expected it.

It would be better than eating by myself, but I don't want to intrude. Besides he probably just offered to be nice. He doesn't really want me there. "I don't know. I don't want to intrude," I spoke right as the elevator doors opened.

"Nonsense, you wouldn't be intruding at all. The more, the merrier," Justin said with a cheery tone and bounce in his step as he exited the elevator. I rolled my eyes. *He is far too chipper for the morning.*

I followed Justin. Seeing as we were going to the same place, I didn't have a way to avoid him. We arrived at the hotel dining area, and sure enough, the rest of Advanced Company had already claimed a table. One of them saw Justin and waved him over. Justin began to approach their table, while I just stood in place, looking for a free table.

Justin paused only a few steps into his trek and turned around. "Are you coming?" he asked.

I looked at Justin and then at the table of boys. I didn't know what to say. Seconds felt like minutes as I quickly tried to make up my mind. *On one hand, I have no desire to eat by myself. On the other hand, I hardly know them. I would be eating with a bunch of strangers.*

I was finally able to fumble out, "No, It's OK. I don't want to be a bother."

"Trust me. We put up with Nick; you aren't a bother," Justin said, as though putting up with Nick was the single hardest task.

I heard a "Hey!" from behind Justin, signaling Nick had heard Justin's quip.

I cracked a small smile at Nick's response. Justin's joke reminded me of something Darren would say, and it was enough to ease my nerves. I smiled at Justin and mustered what small shred of courage I had: "I would love to join you guys."

"Great," he said, turning toward the table. I breathed deeply once he had turned around. *Why do I feel like today is going to be a long day?*

The boys were at a four-person table with two chairs on each side, because they didn't expect another person to join them. I was about to grab a chair, but Justin beat me to it. He pulled up an extra one and put it at the head of the table. I thanked Justin and took my seat.

As soon as Justin sat down, the boys instantly started poking fun at how long it took Justin to get ready. I listened to them tease one another back and forth, all the while briefly glancing around.

The dining area was full of people—anywhere from couples to families—all enjoying each other's company. Everyone's conversations blended into one.

I focused all my attention back to the table, letting the faint mumbles blend into background noise. I listened intently as the boys started talking about a performance they had today.

"Hey, Kinsley you should come," Justin said. I was caught off guard by his suggestion, and I quickly glanced around the table to try and read everyone's expressions. The guys appeared to think it was a good idea, with most of them nodding or smiling.

It occurred to me my parents wouldn't be OK with me leaving the hotel, and I wasn't about to drive somewhere with a group of complete strangers, friendly or not.

"Where is it?" I inquired.

"Here at the hotel," Nick said.

"Oh. When is it?" I was concerned about making my brother's performance.

"The show starts at 3:30. You don't need a ticket. You could watch from backstage," Justin said. I figured I could watch an hour of their performance and then head over to watch Darren.

"I would love to watch you guys perform," I conceded.

Justin smiled victoriously.

"You should come watch our rehearsal!" Tommy said, leaning forward in his chair, enthusiastically awaiting my response.

As much as I wanted to make Tommy happy by saying yes, I couldn't help but feel like I would be in the way. "That's okay. I wouldn't want to disrupt your rehearsal," I said.

Tommy's smile faded. I quickly went to apologize, but Justin cut me off before I could. "You wouldn't be disrupting anything. It's not an official rehearsal. We just wanted one final rehearsal to ourselves before we did the final run-through with the other artists."

That seemed much less intimidating than what I had been thinking. "Oh. I figured it was your final rehearsal," I said as I fiddled with my hands.

When I didn't say anything else, Justin continued, "It would be nice to have another fresh set of eyes on the routine." He definitely knew how to be persuasive.

I finally caved. "Alright, if you're sure I won't be in the way, I would love to watch your rehearsal." I directed my answer and smile in Tommy's direction.

Tommy's excitement snapped back as he pumped his fist in the air and said, "Yes!"

Nick stood up and announced, "I'm gonna go get my food, because thanks to this guy," he pointed at Justin, "I'm starving." Justin rolled his eyes.

Adam, Tommy, and Justin stood up to get their food, and I got up after them. I walked through the buffet line behind Justin. I looked at the wide variety of food: oatmeal and cereal, pancakes and waffles, eggs, bacon and sausage, and hash browns and home-fries. I grabbed a small serving of eggs and a few pieces of bacon—not a ton but enough to satisfy me. I finished getting my food before anyone, so I took it back to the table and went to get a drink.

As I stood in front of the drink machine trying to decide what to get, all of a sudden from right behind me, I heard a loud, "Hey there!" Scared out of my thoughts, I jumped and whipped around to find Justin laughing at my reaction.

Crossing my arms and glaring at him, I scolded, "You know I am not responsible for your injuries if you try that again."

My threat just made him laugh again. "Am I supposed to feel threatened?" he asked, playfully challenging my statement with a cocky grin and raised eyebrow.

"I grew up with two brothers; though she is little but fierce," I said confidently back. Justin gave me a toothy smile and shook his head as he proceeded to get his drink.

I turned back around and quickly filled my glass with orange juice. Everyone returned to the table, and we all started eating.

"Kinsley, do you and your family have any fun plans while you're here?" Adam asked out of the blue.

"Well, my family is working the showcase, and I'll watch my brothers perform, but other than that I have absolutely nothing planned. What about you guys?"

They all took turns talking about their performance that day, and then all the different things they wanted to do over their time at the hotel. It occurred to me that while talking about what they wanted to do, they hadn't mentioned any of their parents or family.

"Are you guys here alone, or did your parents come with you?" I inquired.

"Our manager is here with us, and Nick's mom came as a sort of chaperone," Adam explained.

"Our parents worry less if one of them can come along with us," Justin added.

"That makes sense." I nodded my head in understanding. Another thought popped into my head. "Do you guys only have the one performance?"

"That's basically it. Our manager was able to schedule a meeting with someone who is interested in hiring us for another show. Other than that, we don't have anything. We essentially turned our performance into a vacation," Justin explained.

"Your parents are okay with you all talking a vacation without them?" I asked skeptically.

"We're good kids who don't get into a lot of trouble—but don't have a lot of downtime. They were all for it," Nick said nonchalantly.

I guess that makes sense. I let my curiosity get the better of me. "How long are you guys here for?"

"We're here seven more days, what about you?" Adam said.

That's a weird coincidence. They're here exactly the same amount of time that I am.

"The same, actually," I said.

"Nice! I'm sure we'll see you around a lot then," Justin said with a smile.

Conversation continued to flow smoothly around the table. As we talked, I learned different things about the guys. They were all into sports of some kind. Nick, Justin, and Tommy all liked basketball. Whereas Adam's favorite sport was soccer, and he was of course teased about it "not being a real sport," he was a fan of basketball as well. But soccer remained his first choice.

I was afraid they would ask about my hobbies, so I tried to keep the conversation focused on them. Until Justin decided it was time to learn more about me.

"Where are you from?"

I can answer that. That's a safe enough question. "Do you mean where do I live, or where was I born and raised?" I asked to clarify Justin's question.

Justin shrugged. "Both."

"Born in Michigan. I lived in the same house there 'til I was eight, then moved to California. I'm still currently in California, though we've lived in three completely different cities there. What about you guys?" *It's hard to make friends when you are constantly the "new kid." Fitting in at school is hard enough, let alone when you are continually moving. I wish I had a normal life,* I thought.

I was surprised when Tommy was the first person to answer me. "We live in California too!" His voice was laced with excitement. I smiled at his enthusiasm.

"Have you all lived there long?" I asked.

"Born and raised. We all grew up together in the same town," Justin said. Nick jumped into the conversation.

"We've known each other since we were babies." It came as no surprise to me that they had all been friends for so long. You could see their deep connection in how they talked with each other.

The boys went on to talk about how Nick, Adam, and Justin even went to the same school, they all took dance lessons at the same studio, and hung out on a regular basis. They saw each other all the time.

I was about to ask them what town they lived in when I glanced down at my phone to check the time. It was 10 a.m. Justin noticed I had checked, and asked what time it was.

When I told him, he turned to the others. "What should we do? We only have an hour." Justin said.

"We could all go check out the teen lounge?" Adam said, throwing out an idea. Everyone seemed to think that was an excellent way to kill time. As we rose from the table and embarked toward the lounge, the previous conversation was forgotten.

Chapter 7

I had no clue where we were going, so I walked just slightly behind the boys, buying myself a moment alone. Justin all of a sudden dropped back and fell into step with me.

"So, what do you think of this motley crew?" he asked, giving a slight laugh to his joke.

"If you think this is motley, you should see my brothers and me," I said.

"I find that hard to believe," he said, looking at me skeptically.

I shrugged my shoulders. "Hey, what can I say? I'm full of surprises."

Justin nodded his head in agreement. "That you are."

He paused briefly before continuing. Justin was hesitant when he spoke, as though he was afraid of what my response would be. "Are you looking forward to watching us perform?"

I responded honestly. "You know, I am. When my day started, I thought it was going to be boring with no fun in sight. However, you guys have given me something enjoyable to do."

"Our performances are pretty awesome, if I do say so myself," he said with mock confidence.

I gave a short laugh. "Oh, is that right? I see modesty isn't one of your strong suits," I continued our banter.

"Can't help it when you're great," he retorted.

I laughed before responding, "I think I'll be the judge of that."

Justin smiled. "Well, I can't wait to know what you think," he said as we reached the lounge.

Adam was holding the door open for all of us to enter. I walked into the room and gave a quick look around. It was apparent they had ceased the safari theme in this room. The carpet was light gray with black flecks in it. Three of the walls were charcoal gray. One wall had gray distressed wood paneling running horizontally across it with a TV mounted on the wall. Two black leather couches and a black and gray chair completed it. Despite the dark colors, the room seemed perfectly lit.

I noticed a music system against the far wall and made my way over to examine it. The way it was set up, you could pick any song you wanted or just choose a radio station. While everyone was claiming their seats, I scrolled through the radio stations until I found one that I thought everyone would like.

I considered asking everyone what they wanted to listen to, but for once I thought I should be bold and make a decision. *When it comes to music, I'm usually good at picking stuff everyone likes. The one thing in life I'm comfortable with is music.*

"If you guys don't like the music that's playing, you can change it. I just took a shot in the dark," I said as I walked over to the couch and sat next to Justin. As it turned out, it was the only seat left due to Adam taking the lone chair and Nick and Tommy having sprawled out over one couch.

"No, this music was a great choice," Nick said.

It was quiet for a moment, while everyone took in the room. Adam was the first to break the silence. "Do you have any siblings?" he asked me.

"Yeah, one older brother and one younger. What about you guys?"

Nick was the first to respond. "I'm an only child."

"Maybe that explains why you don't play well with others," Justin teased Nick.

"What's your excuse then?" Nick fired back.

Justin feigned innocence. "I don't know what you're talking about. I get along with everyone." All of us laughed at Justin's quip.

"Whatever helps you sleep at night," Nick said, making it clear he had run out of witty responses and the joking was dying down for the moment.

I decided to continue the previous conversation about siblings. "What about you, Tommy? Any siblings?" I asked.

"One older sister; she's about your age. Maybe a little older. How old are you?"

I answered Tommy's question by telling him I was 14.

"Yeah she's older. She's 15," Tommy said.

"Alright, cool," I said before asking Adam the same question. "Adam, any siblings?"

"I have a twin sister," he said.

"I've always wondered what it would be like to have a twin," I said, thinking about how great and frustrating that must be.

"It's cool, but nothing super special. You have to share your birthday with someone else, and your sibling is in the same grade as you, so that's a little abnormal I guess," Adam said, as though it was nothing.

"Your turn, Justin," Nick said.

"I have two older brothers," Justin said.

That means three boys. His mother raised three boys. "Wow, your mom must have had her hands full when you were younger," I said, amazed.

"I don't know what you're talking about;. we were all angels. See my halo?" Justin pointed to the top of his head.

"Yeah, I see the little horns holding it up," Adam's voice was laced with sarcasm.

"Like you and your sister were any better! Your mom said you and Ashley were always getting into trouble," Tommy countered Adam.

I just kept laughing as the boys continued their banter. The only thing that would stop someone from assuming they were all brothers was their appearance. By the way they all talked with each other, my first guess would have been that they were brothers. *I guess that's what happens when you spend a lot of time with someone.*

After they finished their battle of wits, Justin turned to me. "When I met you, you said you'd heard of us. How did you hear about us?"

I considered the best way to answer this question without lying or revealing too much. "Oh… I think I stumbled across one of your videos on YouTube." *Or I heard they were an up-and-coming group and I wanted to check out their moves and see if I could learn something from their videos. So I may have watched more than one…*

"What did you think?" Tommy inquired.

"The video was good. You guys are talented dancers, " I said genuinely.

"You told me earlier you were a fan of dance. Do you dance?" Justin asked.

My brain went into overdrive searching for an answer that wasn't a lie—but also wouldn't help Justin put all the pieces together. "Well, I enjoy dancing as much as the next person. But I haven't taken any classes, and I'm no good at it. I could never be a professional like you guys," I said, satisfied with my answer.

Justin didn't hesitate to offer, "We could teach you."

How did I know he would say that? I mentally told myself never to bring up the subject of dance with them again—*yeah, cause that will work.*

I was finding the best way to respond when Adam jumped in, "I hate to interrupt and be the party pooper, but we have to head over to rehearsal, or we'll be late."

I was saved by the clock, though it was hard to believe that much time had passed. I looked at the time and saw it was 10:55 a.m. We all stood and headed out for their rehearsal.

Chapter 8

I was inwardly super excited to see their rehearsal; I was bound to learn a thing or two. I made sure to keep my eagerness in check, so I didn't seem like some overexcited fan.

We all trooped through the hotel back towards the conference and performance wing. I was hoping my parents wouldn't see me; otherwise, they would make me sit around and wait with them until my brother's performance.

The only reason they want me at the showcase is they hope I will find some desire to become a dancer or something. That way I will be in the industry like the rest of the family.

They may also want to keep me close out of fear that I will miss Darren's performance. They don't consider that I'm responsible and keep track of time when I have something important to attend—not that my brother would care if I'm on time or not.

The guys stopped and entered into a room, so I figured this was where they had rehearsal. Justin held the door for me again as I stepped through. The room was set up almost exactly like the one for the showcase—with a stage and a bunch of chairs.

The boys made their way up onto the stage. I awkwardly stood near the stage, but far enough from it that I thought I was out of the way.

I didn't know what to do with myself. I felt odd being at someone else's rehearsal. There were a few people who I assumed were the tech crew—walking around and working with the speakers and sound equipment. I made a mental note to stay out of their way.

I jumped when a man clapped his hands together. "OK, let's get started," he said, only then to pause when he noticed me. "Who is this?" he asked as he strode over to me. I awkwardly stood where I was and couldn't bring myself to say any words.

"This is Kinsley. She's a friend of ours. Kinsley, this is Dustin, our choreographer," Justin said, introducing us both and saving me from embarrassing myself.

I thought the practice was going to be just Advanced Company. I 'didn't realize that anyone else would be here other than the boys. I realized my entire body was tense—*I don't like meeting new people.*

"It's nice to meet you, Kinsley." He smiled warmly as he shook my hand.

"You too," I said.

Dustin walked back to the front of the stage. "All right guys, are you ready?" Dustin asked.

The boys nodded their heads and said various yeahs and yeses.

"Okay, show me what you got." With that, he instructed one of the tech guys to play the music, and the routine began.

They were impressive; they all remembered every step. However, the boys had a handful of times when they weren't fully in-sync. They worked on the rough patches, and then ran it one more time to smooth out the timing.

My phone buzzed in my pocket, and I pulled it out to see who it was. I eyed my mom's name on the screen. I stepped out of the room and answered the call, "Hello?"

"Hey Kinsley, I have a short break. Do you want to meet up for lunch?" she asked. I'm not sure if I was more shocked by the fact that Mom had free time or that she thought to spend it with me. I suddenly realized I hadn't answered yet.

"Yes. I would love to!" I said enthusiastically.

"Great. Can you meet me in the dining area at 12:30?" Mom asked.

I didn't hesitate with my answer, "Definitely."

"Okay great. See you in a few," Mom said before hanging up.

As soon as I hung up with her, the door opened, and Justin came out.

"Everything okay?" he asked, concern etched on his face.

"Oh yeah, my mom just wanted to know if I was free to go to lunch with her," I explained.

"Oh, that's cool," Justin said. It occurred to me the boys' rehearsal probably wasn't over, and yet here Justin was talking to me.

"Wait; did you leave in the middle of rehearsal?" I questioned.

"No, we have a five-minute break," he said.

Of course he wouldn't have left in the middle of rehearsal, what a dumb thing to ask. "Oh, okay," was all I came up with in response.

Justin opened the door, and I stepped through to find the rest of Advanced Company sitting on the stage, stretching and talking. Justin jogged off to join them, but I remained by the door.

The choreographer approached me. "How do the boys know you? Do you dance?" he asked with hope in his eyes.

"I just met them, and I only dance for fun. I'm not any good at it. It's just for my enjoyment—nothing more," I said, rambling. *When I'm uncomfortable, I ramble, and when people talk to me about dance, it makes me nervous—because I'm Incognito Moves. I'm always afraid I'll slip up and say something to give it away.*

"The most important thing about dance is that you enjoy it," he said before excusing himself to head to the soundboard.

Once Dustin finished his discussion, he addressed the guys. "OK, Advanced Company; break's over. Let's run your dance one more time."

The guys all stood up, and they started again. Once they completed their routine, I glanced at the time and saw it was 12:25 p.m.

"I have to go meet my mom for lunch," I said as soon as the boys were within speaking distance.

"Thanks for coming to our rehearsal," Tommy said with a wide grin.

"You're welcome." It then dawned on me, I didn't know where I was supposed to go when I came back for their performance. "What do I do about getting back in for your performance?"

Justin quickly shared the location of a door that led to backstage and told me to meet him there at 3:15 p.m.

I said my goodbye and sped to the dining area. I got there precisely at 12:31 p.m., and Mom was nowhere in sight. I settled down at a table for two and waited.

I occupied myself by looking around. There weren't very many people there, so it was relatively quiet. I could make out bits and pieces of the couple's conversation two tables over.

I peered down at the time and saw it was already 12:45 p.m. Just when I thought maybe she wasn't going to show, I caught sight of my mom walking toward the table.

"Sorry I'm late," Mom said apologetically.

"No problem," I said as she took her seat. "How's the showcase been?"

My mom was more than happy to share about the show-case. Her whole demeanor changed when I asked. She went from slightly stressed to happy as a clam. I quickly realized my mistake of asking that question. Part of Mom's precise personality is she doesn't briefly tell stories. She rattles off every last detail to perfection.

On a regular basis, I love to hear my mom recount stories with such precision; but today, I was hoping for some conversation unrelated to the showcase. Nonetheless, I listened to what my mom had to say. *After all, talking to her about the showcase is better than not talking to her at all.*

It wasn't until after we had finished eating that it seemed Mom's lengthy description was nearing completion. I waited with anticipation for her to finish, when all of a sudden her phone started ringing. If it weren't rude to do so, I would have groaned. Mom glanced at the name on the phone and then looked at me apologetically.

Before she could say anything, I said, "Go ahead. Answer it." I had mastered making it seem like an interrupting phone call wasn't a big deal.

I was astonished at how brief Mom's phone call was. Once she hung up, I recognized the look on her face. Before she even let one word out, I felt myself deflate.

"I'm sorry. I have to go back to the showcase," Mom said with a soft tone.

I concealed my disappointment with a smile, "It's OK. I don't mind. Thanks for meeting me for lunch," I said.

Mom returned my smile with a much more genuine one than mine. "My pleasure. I'll see you later," Mom said as she stood up.

Once standing, she suddenly recalled something. "Oh, don't forget about Darren's performance." I just gave a small nod and smile to acknowledge what she said. Without another word, Mom strode off back to the showcase.

"Wouldn't dream of missing it," I mumbled under my breath spitefully.

I glanced down at the time and saw it was 1:50 p.m. *Great, an hour and twenty minutes 'til I meet up with Justin.*

Chapter 9

An hour later, I found myself standing outside the door where Justin said he would meet me. I hadn't knocked yet, because I was early. I occupied myself by thinking about their rehearsal earlier that day. *If they were that good in rehearsal, I can't imagine how great their actual performance will be.*

It dawned on me that Justin had introduced me to their choreographer as a *friend*. I had never considered that they would already think of me as a friend. *I've only known them two days. Not to mention they don't know much about me, and who knows if I'll ever see them after I leave this hotel. I know they live in California, but I still don't know where in California. I could ask them where they live, but there really isn't reason to. It's not like they'll even want to stay in contact with me after this trip. Besides, California is a massive state. The chances of them living close to me or ever seeing me again were slim to none.*

I was snapped out of my thoughts when the door opened to reveal Justin. "You're early," he said with a crooked grin. I smiled back as I quickly took in his appearance. Justin had changed his outfit. I assumed this is what he would perform in. He wore black cargo pants and an army-green shirt, and his shoes were army camo. He finished off the look with a black and camo snapback.

"You are too," I said, knowing it wasn't quite 3:15 p.m.

"I was simply too excited to see you," Justin said with a glint in his eye. Even though I could tell Justin was being sarcastic, it almost seemed like there was slight truth behind his teasing facade. I ignored the thought, thinking I was ridiculous.

Justin opened the door and gestured for me to enter. "After you." I thanked him and advanced through the door. When we reached backstage, the other boys were already there waiting. They all wore similar outfits that matched in color, but each was slightly distinct. Adam was dressed in army-green pants, a black shirt, and black shoes. Nick donned camo pants, an army-green shirt, and army-green shoes—finishing off the look with a black snapback. Last, Tommy had on black pants, a camo shirt, and army-green shoes.

The guys were the opening performance, so I didn't have to wait long until it was time for them to perform. The MC introduced Advanced Company while the boys ran out on stage and got in position for their routine. I'm sure the ear-piercing screams of their fans could be heard out in the lobby. It was a full crowd. If I had to guess, I would say the show was sold out. The majority of the audience members were young teenage girls—no surprises there—though they did have some older fans, and there were plenty of guys in the audience as well.

The music blasted through the speakers, and they began their dance. They were even better than in rehearsal. Not a single step was off. Their performance execution was flawless. The dance was hip-hop, but it had a distinct spin on it. I could describe their style in one-word: *original.*

Their routine was full of energy, which only fueled the crowd's excitement. I watched in awe at how fast they could move. What should look like flailing limbs at the speed they were moving, were precision movements. The tricks and motions they were able to pull off were unbelievable. You didn't have to be a big fan of dance to appreciate the show. The boys had great showmanship, and it was easy to get lost in the routine. They danced with such charisma and energy. You couldn't look away.

The performance ended, and they ran back off the stage, buzzing with excitement.

"You guys were awesome!" I said with awe. They all thanked me.

"We each have small solo performances as well," Adam said, informing me.

"Oh cool, I can't wait to see them." I showed genuine interest.

As I waited in the wings of the stage and watched the other groups and individuals perform, I looked at the time and noticed it was almost 4 p.m. If they didn't perform soon, I would have to miss their solos. Just then, Tommy was announced, and he ran on stage and performed his routine. Then Adam, then Nick, then Justin.

The first three boys' solos were similar in style, yet each somewhat unique. Justin's solo, however, was entirely distinct. His dance was a different style altogether. The first three were strictly hip-hop, but his seemed like hip-hop mixed with something else—possibly contemporary.

When Justin got off stage, he beamed. You could tell he loved dancing, and he was good at it too.

"That was great!" I said. I meant it.

"You liked it?" he asked with hopeful eyes.

"Loved it; you were incredible." Just then, I looked at the time and panicked. *I may be late for my brother's performance.* "Shoot! I have to go. I'll see you guys around," I said as I quickly fled.

I dashed over to the showcase and entered the room that held the main stage. People swarmed the area, so I stood in the back. I thought maybe my brother would catch a glimpse of me and know I was there if I was standing.

They declared they had a special guest who was a returning winner of last year's singing portion. They announced my brother's name, and he came out on stage with his guitar slung around him. Darren had on a black leather jacket with a white T-shirt underneath, dark skinny jeans, and he finished off the look with black leather Converse.

Darren strolled to the microphone with confidence. "It's an honor to be back where it all began. If it weren't for this showcase, I wouldn't be where I am today. I'm going to sing one of the new songs I wrote. I hope you all like it." Once he finished his speech, he began strumming his guitar and started to sing. I realized it was my favorite of all his songs.

Darren looked so at home on stage, like it was where he was meant to be. He was so confident in his abilities. *I want that. I don't want to be concerned about what others think. I want to be able to be confident in myself—and not have doubts—like him.* He finished his song, which brought me out of my thoughts. I clapped as loudly as I could. I was so proud of my brother.

I left the main room and quickly found the backstage area with a room reserved for returning performers. I knocked, and Darren opened the door.

"You were amazing!" I complimented him as I gave him a big hug. To my amazement, he hugged me back with no rejection or complaint.

"Thanks, Kins," he said in response.

"You know, that's my favorite song you've written," I said with a smile.

Darren nodded his head. "Yeah? I picked the song for you."

My smile beamed ear to ear. "Thank you, that means a lot to me."

My brothers never cease to baffle me. Just when I think they couldn't care less about who I am or what I do, they go and do something sweet like this.

"Well, that was all I had to do for today. Do you want to go back to the room?" Darren said.

"What about Mom and them?" I asked with furrowed eyebrows.

"They already stopped by. They were all dragged away to help with something else and said just to meet them upstairs," Darren explained.

"Then what are we doing standing around? Let's head upstairs."

We meandered to the elevator, teasing each other the entire way in typical sibling fashion. When we reached the lobby, people looked at us like we were crazy. We were laughing so loudly and making so much noise—which only made us laugh more.

Just seconds after we entered the hotel room, Darren's phone rang. I could tell from the way he answered it was one of his friends. He departed to his room to finish his conversation.

Within seconds, I'm forgotten. Great. Now what am I supposed to do?

Chapter 10

I trudged into my room and logged onto my YouTube profile. I observed that I had new subscribers and a lot of new comments on my video—or should I say, Incognito's video? I always read every comment. Some were hateful, but some were good; it was kind of 50/50. They ranged from, "That was great," and "Amazing skill," to things like, "No technique at all," and "You're not that good."

I sighed and logged off YouTube to pull up Twitter. I followed a lot of my fans back on Twitter, because I liked to talk to them and see what they thought: What could I improve? What songs did they want me to dance to? I learned stuff like that.

While online, I got a direct message from a fan. I opened the message. "Hey Incognito Moves, I loved the last video you put up; it was amazing! Thanks for using my recommendation of a song!"

I smiled and typed back, "You're more than welcome. I love that song, and you're one of my most supportive fans, so when you suggested that song, there was no way I wasn't going to dance to it."

I logged off Twitter when I heard voices in the family room. I closed my laptop and wandered to follow the sounds.

"Hey," I said to no one in particular.

"How's your day been so far?" my dad asked.

"Um, pretty good, I guess. You guys?"

"Very busy," Mom said. By now, Ty had already exited into his room, and it was just my parents and me in the family room.

I looked at my phone, and it was 5:20 p.m. Since there wasn't much going on here, I figured they wouldn't care if I went out for a bit.

"Hey, would you guys mind if I walked around the hotel some?" I asked.

"No, that's fine," Dad said.

"Thanks," I said. I dashed into my room and grabbed the book I was in the middle of reading, in case I found a spot to sit down and chill. I grabbed my room key, put my headphones in, and walked out the door.

I walked past the eating area and decided I would see how crowded the teen area was. Upon entering, I was surprised that no one was there. I took my headphones out, plopped onto the couch, and started reading my book. I was already half-way through it and was getting to the best part.

I could hear muted voices right outside the door. People were coming to use the lounge. *There goes my peace and quiet.* I had been in there first, so I didn't feel the need to move. The door opened, and I didn't bother to look up. I kept my nose buried in my book and just tried to ignore the people, hoping they would depart.

The group got quiet all of a sudden. I figured they were looking at me, but I didn't care, since I always tended to get bizarre looks while reading. *What normal kid wants to read while on vacation?*

All of a sudden someone snatched my book out of my hands. "Hey!" I exclaimed as I glared at the culprit. *That was so rude.*

"Whatcha reading?" the culprit asked with a cheeky grin. It, of course, was none other than Justin.

"I have a bad habit of running into you guys, don't I?" I said, snatching my book from Justin's hands.

They all smiled.

"Seems like you just can't get enough of us," Nick said with his signature smirk.

I laughed. "Um, I believe I was here first. If anything, you guys can't stay away from me," I fired back.

"Is that so?" Justin asked with a raised eyebrow.

"Yep, seems that way to me." Justin smiled and shook his head.

I was about to open my book and begin reading again when Tommy interrupted. "Let me get this straight, you have free time, and you willingly chose to read?" he asked, bewildered.

I set my book down. "Is that a crime?" I asked.

"I don't get why anyone would want to torture themselves any more than school does. Why would you read for fun?" Nick said, contorting his face to show his disgust at reading.

Before I could answer, Adam spoke up. "Some people enjoy reading. They think it's fun."

I nodded in agreement. "See? He gets it," I said pointing at Adam.

Tommy shrugged, saying, "I will never understand the appeal of reading."

We talked for a while until Nick blurted out, "We should all go to the indoor water park." Tommy's face lit up with excitement as he bounced up and down in his seat. The others didn't seem to oppose Nick's idea.

"Why not?" Justin said. I assumed they were talking about just them going, so I remained put and opened my book to start reading again.

The guys all stood up, but Tommy paused before heading for the door. "Aren't you coming?" he asked as though it had been implied I was going with them.

"Oh, I thought it was just your group. I figured you'd all had enough of me by now," I said half-jokingly. Nick rolled his eyes.

"Yeah right, are you coming or not?" Nick asked, brushing off my comment.

I glanced at Justin and Adam to make sure they didn't seem to care either. I decided that going to the water park seemed like a fun idea.

"If you guys don't care, then I'll tag along. I'll get my swimsuit on and meet you guys down there," I said, standing up.

"Cool, we'll see you down there," Justin said before walking out the door.

I walked out of the room after they all did, went up to my family's hotel room, and used my key card to get in.

"Back so soon?" Dad asked as soon as I got through the door.

"Yeah, I came up to change into my swimsuit. I decided to go to the water park."

"Okay, be careful," Mom said.

"I will," I said. I changed into my swimsuit and cover-up. I grabbed my towel, book, phone, and headphones and threw them into a bag to bring with me. I transitioned into the family room.

"Okay, I'll see you guys later," I said as I exited out the door and voyaged to the indoor water park.

Chapter 11

Once I got to the water park, I perused the area and didn't see Advanced Company. I picked a row of chairs poolside. I settled my stuff beside my chair and laid down with my book. I happened to glance up a minute later, and I saw the boys wandering into the park. I waved my hand so they would notice me, and once they did, they started walking over.

I bookmarked my page and put my book back in my bag. They all placed their stuff on chairs of their choice.

"You guys ready to have some fun?" Nick enthusiastically asked. We all nodded our heads. "Well, what are we waiting for? Let's go." He waved for all of us to follow him.

The guys started to march off, so I took off my cover-up and followed. We all decided to start with one of the body slides, so we didn't have to wait for inner tubes.

"Kinsley, what had you leaving in such a rush after our performance earlier?" Adam asked, his curiosity getting the better of him.

"Oh yeah, I should have told you guys why. My brother was performing in a showcase, and I wanted to watch. My parents wanted me to be there. I was a little late, but I got to see my brother sing, so it was all good." He looked satisfied with my answer.

As we approached the top of the slide, I got an idea: "We should all race."

The boys were quick to agree. "Winner should get something," Nick suggested.

"Like what?" I asked, not sure what he meant by that.

"I don't know, but something to up the stakes, make it feel like a real competition," Nick said with a spark in his eye.

We all considered Nick's proposal for a minute.

"What about winner picks the next slide we go on?" Adam inquired. Everyone seemed to be pleased with that idea.

"Since we can't all race at the same time, the person who wins the first race gets to pick the slide we do next. After that, the winner from the second set of racers can pick what slide we do," Adam said, making sure the details were crystal clear.

"Who races first?" Justin asked.

"I want to go in the first group," Tommy eagerly volunteered.

"What about Adam and me?" Nick inquired.

"Okay, it's settled then. Tommy, Nick, and Adam for the first group; and Justin and I for the second group," I said, making sure I got the groups straight.

We finally reached the top, and it was the first group's turn. Once the other boys had walked away to go down the slide, Justin asked me, "Who do you think will win?"

"Probably Nick. Who do you think will win?" I asked.

"I think Adam has a pretty good shot," he stated.

I just smiled. "Nah, I'm pretty confident it will be Nick."

Justin shook his head no and commented back, "No way. It's gonna be Adam by far."

I smirked. "Well, I guess we'll just see who's right."

"I guess we will," Justin said, returning the smirk.

It was our turn to race. We got in position. I was well aware I wasn't going to win the race. I was never fast down slides.

The lifeguard gave us the all-clear, and I launched myself down the slide. A small rush of adrenaline rushed through me as I was propelled down the slide. I had chosen one of the enclosed slides; they seemed more fun to me than the open ones. I couldn't see much of anything, so I didn't know what was coming next. Each twist and turn was a surprise, only adding to the fun.

The slide all of a sudden got increasingly brighter, and I knew I was nearing the opening. I held my breath as I plunged into the cool water.

I stood up and saw Justin was already ahead of me, making his way to the exit of the splash pool. He beat me just like I expected. I finally arrived at the group of guys.

"Who won out of you three?" I asked, gesturing to Adam, Nick, and Tommy.

Tommy and Adam simply pointed to Nick, and as typical, Nick gestured toward himself with both thumbs and confidently said, "The one and only."

I smiled and shook my head slightly at his goofiness.

"Clearly Justin won out of you two," Tommy said.

"Well, I can't be better than him at everything. I have to let him have a few wins." I poked fun at Justin.

"Oh thank you; you're so kind." Justin played along with my joke.

"So Nick, where to next?" I asked.

Nick thought for a moment and looked around. "Um… how about the wave pool?" We all began the trek in that direction, with Justin and me slightly lagging behind. I was smiling, or more accurately, smirking.

"I don't trust that smile," Justin said wearily. He continued, "What is making you smile?"

"Oh, you know—that I was right," I said matter-of-factly.

Justin shook his head, amused. "I figured that was why you were smirking like that."

"What smirk? I'm not smirking," I said sarcastically.

"You're enjoying this a little too much," Justin said.

"Maybe just a little."

We arrived at the wave pool; the others had run ahead and were already out splashing and playing in the surf. Justin started to run in to catch up with them. I just slowly shuffled in.

Most people love the wave pool; I do not. I feel like I nearly drown every time, and I'm not sure why, since I'm a pretty decent swimmer. I think it's just all the people and the inner tubes over-crowding the pool. I always end up getting trapped.

Most of my friends and family nag me and say, "You're being overdramatic. You haven't ever actually drowned—just nearly." Yes, because that makes it so much better.

I'm sure this time will be different. After all, I'm sure I can hold my breath longer and swim better than last time.

I got above my waist in the water and could tell by how weak the waves were that they had just started to build momentum. I walked a little farther in until I was pretty much blocked by inner tubes and couldn't get any farther. I could barely see between the two inner tubes in front of me, but I made out Justin waving for me to join them. I summoned up all my courage and convinced myself everything would be fine.

I held my breath and swam under the two inner tubes. I miraculously got to the other side safely. *Maybe this time really will be different.* I swam to the guys, but it was hard to stay near them because of how many inner tubes were scattered across the water. The waves had gotten much more intense. I found it hard to keep my head above the water, since I couldn't touch the bottom. The waves rolled over my head, and the inner tubes shoved into me constantly.

A wave dunked me under the water and simultaneously pushed an inner tube over me, so I couldn't come up for air. As I reached for the surface and tried to open my eyes for seconds at a time, I registered that I was under a group of inner tubes. I couldn't get out of the trap due to the waves and the fact that some people had their feet through the inner tube holes and were kicking at me.

I remained calm and focused on holding my breath while trying to figure a way out. All of a sudden, I felt someone grab my arms and pull me out from under the inner tubes. I surfaced and gasped for air, trying to catch my breath.

Chapter 12

I nearly drowned yet again. Typical. It appears my hatred for the wave pool continues.

Once I had semi-caught my breath, I was able to observe my surroundings. I noticed I had been brought a little shallower so I could stand, and the waves weren't going above my head. To my surprise, it was Justin and Adam who had pulled me out. A lifeguard had come over at the first sign of the commotion, but Adam and Justin had beat them to the rescue.

The lifeguard made sure I was okay before returning to her post. Her lecture about how to avoid these situations only added to the initial humiliation of the accident. I politely nodded my head, taking in everything she had to say. Once the lifeguard headed back to her station, I turned to Adam and Justin.

"Thanks," I said as I fiddled with my hands.

"No problem; we're just glad you're okay." Justin's voice was laced with concern.

"I've never liked the wave pool." I looked down at my hands. I couldn't look at Justin and Adam. I was embarrassed by the fact that they had to save me.

"I understand that," Adam said. "It's not my favorite thing either. I've almost drowned once or twice as well. It's a common thing." That made me feel slightly less embarrassed, since it didn't only happen to me.

We saw a male lifeguard and the other guys coming towards us, with Tommy coughing and trying to catch his breath. "Caught under the inner tubes?" I asked. They nodded their heads. "I know how that is." The lifeguard made sure Tommy was okay and gave familiar instructions to those I'd heard.

Once the lifeguard left to his post, we all agreed to do something else. We didn't want another near-drowning episode. Trudging out of the wave pool, we didn't know where to go next.

"Justin won the race between us. He gets to pick what we do next," I said, reminding everybody of the deal.

Justin thought for a moment. "I saw they had a bodyboarding thing. Why don't we try that? Unless you aren't up for it?" He directed the second part to me. He wasn't challenging me. His voice was sincere.

It's kind of him to be concerned, but they don't need to baby me.

"It's nice of you to be concerned, but I am perfectly fine," I said, making sure it was apparent that I could handle myself.

We all started to head toward a ride coined the Wave-rider—which simulated bodyboarding or surfing. While in line, we watched others try one by one. Some would just stay on their stomachs, some on their knees, and others would try it standing up.

After a while, the lifeguard called the next person, and it was Justin. Justin stood at the top of the ride with his board. He dove forward down the slight incline and landed belly-first on his board. He got to his knees in a flash. I watched as Justin proceeded to spin the board 180 degrees while remaining on it.

Why does he have to be so good at everything?

Apparently, I wasn't the only one who was irritated by Justin's skill. Tommy voiced what we all were thinking, "Why does he have to make everything look so easy?"

"I know, right?" Adam said.

I stayed quiet as I watched Justin. I had anticipated he'd try to stand, since he had gotten to his knees so effortlessly. But he didn't. He remained on his knees and continued to try different tricks. Despite Justin continuously whipping the board around, he didn't fall off.

Adam was next. He dove onto his board, and just like Justin, he got to his knees in an instant; but he stayed on his knees. Adam tried a trick or two—but nothing quite as adventurous as Justin.

Nick went after Adam, and I was certain, knowing how much he liked to show off, he would get to his feet. But like Adam and Justin, he stayed on his knees. Nick was impressive. He managed to complete three full spins while traveling to the left across the wave, then he cut back across the wave again. As Nick tried to complete one more final whip of the board, he lost his balance. He couldn't regain control and wiped out.

Tommy stayed on his stomach, not wanting to chance a fall off the board. Ever on his stomach, he was able to weave the board back and forth across the wave.

After watching people get to their feet earlier, I decided I wanted to attempt standing up. Not that this was a smart decision, but it looked fun. Plus, I had always wanted to learn how to surf, and at this very moment, this was the closest I was going to get.

I took a deep breath before launching myself down the incline into the rushing water. I got to my knees rather easily, but when I tried to stand up, that was a different story. I managed to make it to my feet but then instantly lost my balance and fell off. I felt some minor pain during my wipeout, but not too much.

I got to the boys, and they all stared at me in disbelief.

"That. Was. Awesome!" Tommy paused at each word for emphasis.

Adam seemed to agree. "Yeah, that was pretty impressive."

"I fell; it wasn't that cool," I said, darting my eyes to the ground.

"You fell, but at least you tried. We were all too chicken to even try," Justin said. "Why am I not surprised you have more courage than all of us?"

"I should have tried to stand. I bet I could have stayed up longer," Nick said, unamused that someone one-upped him. We all laughed at Nick's pouting face.

"Whatever you need to tell yourself," Justin said as he patted Nick's shoulder.

"Where to next?" I asked, changing the subject.

"Why don't we just go to one of the normal pools?" Adam said.

Everyone agreed. Once there, Tommy and Adam jumped straight in, not wasting any time. I was walking next to the pool, trying to decide whether I wanted to use the steps or just dive straight in, when Justin came up beside me and attempted to push me in. Having two brothers, I was expecting someone to do such a thing. As I started to fall, I grabbed Justin's arm and pulled him in with me.

Nick was on the side of the pool, laughing at the fact that I pulled Justin in. "Oh, you think it's funny? I can bring you in too," Justin said with a warning glare. Nick immediately jumped in, so Justin wouldn't get out and try to push him in. I laughed at the fact Nick would rather jump in than give someone else the satisfaction of pushing him in.

All of a sudden, I felt someone grab my legs and pull me underwater. I surfaced, only to discover Adam as the culprit. All the guys were laughing.

"Oh, you want to go?" I threatened Adam.

My comment made him laugh more. "Like you could take me—!" Before he could finish, I dunked him underwater in mid-sentence.

Now it was my turn to laugh. I crossed my arms. "You were saying?" I asked smugly. Adam threw his hands up in surrender.

I spotted a roped off area of the pool set aside as a floating obstacle course. The goal was to make it across these big plastic lily pads and logs. The logs and lily pads were chained to the bottom of the pool, so they didn't drift off; but the chain was long enough that they could still move enough to make getting across difficult. A rope net suspended overhead to hold onto while maneuvering across.

The boys noticed what I was staring at right as someone fell off of a lily pad. "We should all try it," Nick said. We all thought it sounded like it could be fun, so we climbed out of the pool and stood in line. Only one little kid was in front of us. He went and got all the way across, making it look easy.

"Who's first?" the lifeguard asked.

"Let me show you how it's done." Nick spoke in his usual cocky way. He swaggered up to do the course first. Nick grabbed the overhead rope net and stepped onto the first lily pad. Then he moved onto the next one and nearly fell in the water but managed to regain his balance. Next was a log. Nick positioned his right foot on the log and kept his left on the lily pad. The log started to turn by the pressure of his foot, and before he did the splits, he let go of the rope and fell in.

"Oh! Really good job, Nick. Now I know exactly what NOT to do," Tommy said, making Nick scowl.

Tommy attempted next. He made it past the first log but then fell off on the second one. Adam almost made it to the end but fell off at the third and final log. Getting across was more difficult than it seemed; strength was needed, but so was good balance.

Justin was the last of the boys to try. He had offered for me to go first, but I politely declined. Justin made it as far as Tommy had, but then he fell in.

"You've got my vote," the lifeguard said to me.

I gave a short laugh. "Thanks. I think I figured out the problem. They all made the mistake of trying to do it too quickly. It's better to take your time on things like this," I said, hopeful that this revelation would get me to the end. The lifeguard smiled but didn't tell me whether I was right or not.

In studying the course of floating lily pads and logs, I diverted my attention to the suspended rope net. *Okay, I can do this. I can do this. Just because the boys had trouble doesn't mean I will… Who am I kidding? If they can't do it, I can't do it. No, I'm capable of this. I just need to concentrate and take my time. Slow and steady wins the race,* I thought as I reached for the suspended rope net.

I hesitantly lifted my right foot onto the first lily pad. I was able to get my left foot to the next floating piece with ease. When I got to the log, I stretched my foot to about its center, so it wouldn't turn or drift. I was successful in bringing both feet to the log. I made it all the way to the last log, using the same tactic as on the first one; but when I tried to get to the final lily pad, the log and lily pad started to separate.

I nearly did the splits, but since I was rather flexible—thanks to dancing—my maneuver didn't hurt. I used my strength to pull myself up on the rope net—forcing the two floating obstacles back together.

I made it to the final lily pad. As I was moving my right foot to the final platform, the lily pad started to drift away. I knew my best option was to jump the remaining gap. I pushed myself off the lily pad and just barely got my foot to the platform. Just as I was about to fall back into the water, Justin grabbed my hand and pulled me forward, saving me from landing in the pool. I was greeted with high-fives from all the guys.

"How'd that not hurt?" Tommy asked, amazed.

"It pays to be flexible," I said. "Which reminds me, you all have terrible balance and flexibility for dancers."

"Well, you have incredible flexibility for a non-dancer," Justin said. Mental alarm bells went off in my head. *Is he implying he knows I'm a dancer?*

Thankfully Nick cut in. "Justin, I think you finally found someone who is good at everything, just like you," he said half-jokingly.

"I'm hardly good at everything. You should hear me sing or watch me play baseball, then you'll take that back," I said. The boys chuckled.

We started talking about water slides and decided to go down two more slides and then be done for the day. As we waited in line, we talked and joked the entire time. I was thankful that the conversation stayed at surface stuff and away from the topic of dance. As cool as the guys seemed, I wasn't ready to share any of my secrets with them. *After all, once I leave the hotel, it's not like I'll seem them again,* I thought to myself.

After enjoying the two slides, we returned to our stuff. I checked my phone and noted I had no texts from my parents, so I was in the clear. I read the time and saw it was 7:30 p.m. *Wow, it didn't feel like we were here that long.*

Right as I was about to sit, my phone sounded. It was a text from my dad saying, "Hey, princess, once you see this we would like you to come up to the room." I responded that I would be up in just a few.

"Well, I have to go. I was summoned." I announced my departure.

"We should probably be getting back too," Adam said.

We all gathered our stuff and headed out. When we arrived at the elevator, they pressed their floor number, and I pressed mine. Everyone was quiet, which was surprising for the boys. There was a slight tension hanging in the air at the suspense of parting ways. I enjoyed getting to hang out with them, and I was a little sad at the idea of going back to my room.

Why am I sad? Why do I even care? I guess it's because when I'm with them, it's easy and generic, even with keeping my secret. I didn't have that with a lot of people. I'm not sure why I had it with them. The ding of the elevator signaling it had arrived at my floor tugged me out of my thoughts.

"I'll see you guys around," I said as I stepped off the elevator.

Chapter 13

When I entered the room, no one was in the family room. That meant everyone was in their rooms. I walked to my parents' room and knocked on the door.

"Come in," I heard Dad say. I opened the door.

"Just letting you know I'm back," I said.

"Okay. We're going to go to dinner soon, so get ready," Mom said.

"Okay," I said as I shut the door.

I moved to my room, set my bag down on my bed, and got ready for dinner. I didn't dress in anything really nice—just jeans and a random T-shirt I had brought.

I'm not in the mood to put effort into what I look like.

I laid down on my bed and decided to go on my personal Twitter account to kill some time. I was on my computer for only a short period when I heard my mom say it was time to go to dinner.

A restaurant was connected to the hotel, so we didn't have to drive anywhere. Dinner was super enjoyable. We joked and enjoyed each other. For a moment, it didn't feel like we were at a showcase. It felt like an actual family vacation.

I looked intently at each family member. They all seemed perfect—unlike me. I was the odd one out in my family. But it wasn't because I wasn't in the industry; it was because I thought I was so messed up. *I mean none of them have problems talking to strangers, stage fright, fear of rejection, insecurities, anxiety, or anything like that,* I told myself. *They all have their lives together—even Ty. and he's younger than me. I'm just here spinning my wheels, stuck between faceless fame and someone with a face but no real identity.*

I was snapped from my train of thought when everyone stood to return to the room. Upon entering the room, it was as though a light switch was flipped when Ty out of the blue exclaimed, "We should watch a movie!"

"I like the sound of that," Darren added his input.

"Okay, what do you want to watch?" Mom inquired.

Oh no, here we go. This is going to take forever, I thought. I flopped down on the couch next to my dad, as I watched Ty and Darren bicker about what to watch. They couldn't agree on any movie, and when they finally did, Mom rejected it.

I noticed that my dad had stayed silent like I had. *I wonder if that's where I get it.* I leaned over to my dad, sitting next to me on the couch.

"No opinion?" I asked.

"More like I'm smart enough not to get in the middle of this," he said back in a whisper, so the rest of the family wouldn't hear. I stifled a laugh.

"I guess that makes us two the smart ones," I said with a smile.

"I guess so," he said, returning my smile.

Eventually, they came to terms with what to watch. They all finally agreed on watching some comedy action film I had never heard of that appeared to be mild enough for Mom and Ty yet had enough action that Darren was okay with the pick.

I didn't pay much attention to the movie. I kept drifting in and out of my thoughts. I couldn't get fully engaged.

Just when I would start to focus, my thoughts dragged me off again. I was thinking about my revelation at dinner. It was like I was living with a split personality. *One side of me wants not to care about what people think, but the other half wants nothing more than to be liked. Am I the only one who feels this way?*

The movie ended, drawing me from my thoughts. I looked over to find Ty already asleep. My dad got up and carried Ty to his room. Darren followed. Mom and Dad decided to go to bed because they had to wake up early, and they were both exhausted.

When the coast was clear, I went into my room, and grabbed my bag. I threw in something comfortable to dance in, my video camera and speaker, my phone, my room key, and my mask. I rode the elevator down to the lobby. It seemed like I'd spent a lot of time in that elevator recently, transitioning between different roles and situations. I remembered the slight tension at my parting with Advanced Company.

I wonder what they are doing. I shook the thought from my head. *It doesn't matter.*

I started toward the conference wing. As I cut across the lobby, it was almost deserted, except for one couple checking in at the desk.

In the conference wing, I entered the bathroom and changed into my dance clothes. I didn't put my mask on yet, since no one was around. I returned to the same room I'd danced in previously. I entered and flipped on the lights. I crossed over to the far wall and placed my stuff down in a tidy heap.

I set up my speaker and camera. I listened for any sound of someone near. When there wasn't even a squeak, I reached into my bag and pulled out my mask. The empty eyes stared back at me. I lifted my mask to my face and once again dawned the image of Incognito. I walked in front of my camera, introduced myself, and as usual, stated what song I was dancing to.

I stepped back and began to dance. This dance was contemporary. I had envisioned a routine to this song a while ago and was just now getting the chance to try it out. I moved with fluidity and grace, letting the music wash over me and take me away.

When I dance, there's no way to explain the feeling. It's like the whole world just melts away, and it's just me, the music, and all my raw emotions. There's nothing like it. I forget all that's going on in my life as I'm transported to a different world. It seems like the only time my mind is quiet is when I dance.

I finished, said goodbye to my audience, and turned off my camera. My mind flashed back to Advanced Company's show and Darren's performance. Their crowds were energetic; mine was stagnant. They performed for real people you could see and hear; my audience sat somewhere else in the world, hidden behind a screen.

Just like me, my audience is invisible, and I like it better that way...At least I think I do.

I sighed and returned the camera to my bag. As I picked up my bag and turned around to leave, I saw a figure just standing there. I jumped, startled by his presence. I calmed a tiny bit when I saw who it was. It was Justin...again. Somehow he seemed to know where I was at all times.

"You know, I'm not responsible for your injuries if you scare me like that again," I said, wringing my hands together. Even though it was only Justin, my body was on high alert. I was scanning his expression for any sign that he'd seen me unmasked.

He chuckled. "Sorry, I didn't know what to do. You ran away last time." He ran his hand across the back of his neck.

I wasn't sure what to say. "Sorry about that. I'm not used to meeting fans," I said, hoping that was enough to explain my earlier behavior.

"I'm sure you also didn't want to run the risk of me figuring out who you were," he said.

I nodded, afraid to speak.

"That was amazing," Justin complimented after a short pause.

"Thanks," was all I said in response.

That's it. That's all I can think to say. I seriously need to get better at this. I racked my brain trying to figure out something—anything—to talk about, but it was like my mind was frozen.

"I'm probably overstepping, but do you mind if I ask if you'll ever show people who you are?" he asked.

"Probably not." Justin was taken aback by my quick and simple answer.

"Oh... What if someone figures it out? What then?" he asked, letting his curiosity get the best of him.

I let out a short, sharp laugh, "I doubt anyone will ever figure out who I am. There's no distinguishing factor in my videos or anything that points to my identity. I'm not sure why people want to know so badly. I'm just your average girl."

I could tell he was taking in what I had said before he responded. But before he could ask any more questions, I continued. "It's late. I should be getting back to my room." I started to walk by him, but he stopped me by gently grabbed my forearm.

"Can I ask one more question?" he said as he dropped his hand from my arm. I sighed and turned around to meet his eyes.

"Yes."

"What are you at this hotel for?" he asked. I could see in his eyes his brain was trying to put the pieces together.

"It's a long story," I said, hoping to get him to stop asking questions.

I didn't want to lie; but I also couldn't tell him the truth, or he would know who I was.

I have probably said too much already.

"I have time," he said with a warm smile.

"Sorry, I don't," I said as I left the room. I was walking down the hall when just a few seconds later, I heard him call out.

"Wait!" I heard footsteps behind me, but I turned the corner and quietly entered the room right next to me and locked the door. I let out a breath I had been holding. I waited in the room a while until I figured he was gone.

I cracked the door open and peered out. Thankfully, he wasn't there. I returned to the bathroom to change back into my normal clothes and finally started the voyage to my room.

I know I was completely rude. However, if I tell him why I'm at the hotel without lying, he will put two and two together and figure out who I am—if he hasn't figured that out already. It was even ruder to run away, but for some reason, I can't lie to him. I panicked.

I entered the hotel room quietly, so I wouldn't wake anyone up. I stealthily made it to my room and gently closed the door, not making a peep. I flopped on my bed and let out a heavy sigh. I was still in my dance clothes. I knew I should get up and change into my pajamas, but I was too tired to move.

If my parents come in and see me in exercise clothes, they will be confused and probe me with questions until they get a sufficient explanation. I don't want that.

However, my exhaustion won over any logical argument I used to motivate myself to get up and change, so I remained where I was.

<h1 style="text-align:center">Chapter 14</h1>

I woke up the next morning to find myself still in my clothes from the previous night. I remembered I had come home and flopped on my bed without changing. I realized I must have fallen asleep. I was eternally grateful that my parents hadn't come in. I swiftly changed and got ready for the day.

Amid brushing my teeth, I caught a glimpse in the mirror of my bare wrist. My eyes widened, and my toothbrush slipped out of my hand and clattered onto the counter. A wave of panic settled on me. I frantically searched the small bathroom, and when I came up empty-handed, I rushed to my room—all the while thinking, *it can't be gone. It must be here.*

I flung my door open and tore my room apart looking for it, but like in the bathroom, came up empty-handed. It then occurred to me I'd gone to the water park the day before. *Did I remove it for that or not?* A deep sinking feeling settled in my stomach. *It's lost for good. I'm never gonna get it back. I can't believe it. That bracelet meant the world to me, and in the blink of an eye, it's gone. Of course I would lose the bracelet. I'm such an idiot. If only I had paid more attention or… If I was mom. Mom wouldn't have lost it,* I thought. I realized the search was useless and trudged back to the bathroom weighted with guilt.

Trying my best to move on, I emerged from the bathroom and made my way to the family room to find Darren watching TV.

"Who all is still here?"

"Just me. The others went down to the showcase already," Darren said. I sighed.

"Okay, do you want to go to breakfast with me?" I asked, hoping that breakfast would take my mind off losing my bracelet.

"Sure." He turned off the TV and stood up.

We departed to the lobby to eat. Once at the dining area we went on the hunt for a seat. As I glanced around for an open table, I saw Advanced Company, but they hadn't noticed me. Since I was with Darren, I didn't wave or try to get their attention. Darren pointed out an open table, and we sat down.

"I'm going to get my food," I said as I headed to the buffet line. I filled my plate with eggs and bacon. I decided today I would splurge and have a pancake. I was on vacation, after all. I sat my food down at our table and went to get my drink.

I reached the drink machine, and Adam happened to come up beside of me.

"Hey," he said.

"Hey," I replied, not sure what to say once again.

"You want to hang with us later?" he asked.

"Um, probably. I'll have to see what I have today," I said, before we both parted ways back to our tables.

I started to eat my breakfast as Darren sat down from getting his drink. I smiled when I saw his glass had orange juice in it. Preference in favorite breakfast beverage was about the only thing Darren and I had in common.

"Was yesterday all you had to do in the showcase?" I asked. He shook his head as he finished chewing his bite of food. "No, they think they're also going to use me at their masquerade ball as entertainment. Plus some classes or something like that. I don't know. I just go where I'm told."

"That's cool," I said.

The rest of breakfast mainly consisted of passing witty banter back and forth. The light conversation cheered me up and helped me to not focus on losing my bracelet.

Darren and I don't ever have a lot of one on one time together, but when we do I enjoy it. I can always count on Darren to keep me laughing.

I finished my meal before Darren.

"I'm going to go over to the conference wing, I think. See what's going on and see if I can find Mom and Dad," I said standing up.

"Okay, see you later," Darren said.

Back at the showcase wing, I entered the backstage area. As I approached Rachel in the hall to ask where my parents were, she was conversing with someone and didn't seem happy.

"What do you mean, *they can't get here*?" she frantically asked.

"All they said is that they're not able to make it. That something came up," the other person replied.

"Great! What am I supposed to do now? How am I supposed to get a dance group this last minute?!" I had been standing, waiting to talk to her.

"Can I help you?" she asked, trying to calm herself down and go back to her sweet self, but failing miserably.

"Actually, I think I may be able to help you," I said, as the other girl took her opportunity to walk away.

Rachel looked very confused at my answer. "How so?" she hesitantly asked.

I hoped to clarify my original answer. "I heard you're in need of a dance group?"

"Yes, how does that pertain to you?" she asked with furrowed eyebrows.

"What would you say if I told you I could get you a dance group?"

Rachel started walking and waved for me to follow her. I obeyed and fell into step with her. "I would say you were crazy. No one would be willing at such last minute," Rachel said.

"It happens that I met a dance group that had a performance at this hotel, so they could perform—if they agree, that is," I offered.

Rachel immediately came to a stop, and her entire demeanor changed at the possibility of getting someone to perform. "What group?" she asked with a glimmer of hope in her eyes.

"Ever heard of Advanced Company?" I asked.

"Yes, actually I have. You're saying they're here at the hotel? You could get them to perform today, at 4:15 at the dance portion?" Rachel eagerly awaited my response.

"Most likely. I'm sort of, kind of, friends with them. I'm sure they wouldn't mind helping."

"If you could get them, you would be a lifesaver," Rachel said, somewhat excited.

"I'll see what I can do, but no promises." I made sure I didn't set her hopes too high.

"Can I have your phone number to follow up with you?" Rachel asked, handing me her phone to put my information into. "We exchanged texts so we'd have one another's numbers.

"Thank you. I owe you one," Rachel said as she walked off.

Don't thank me yet. They still have to say yes. I hope they say yes. The showcase needs them, plus it would be nice if I could contribute something to the showcase. I sighed. *Now if only I knew where they were.*

I first went to the dining area to see if they were still there, but of course, I wouldn't be so lucky. I trekked over to the teen lounge. *Let's hope they're here.* Opening the door, of course the room was empty. I slumped down on the couch in defeat, trying to decide where to check next. I got up and thought maybe to explore around the hotel and see if I could find them.

How creepy; I'm hunting down a group of guys I barely know. I'm ridiculous. Hey, it's for a business reason. I stepped through the door to exit the teen room and nearly ran into Advanced Company. *What luck!*

"I've been looking for you guys," I said. *That wasn't desperate sounding at all.* I mentally face-palmed.

Now that I was standing face to face with them, I realized how much of a long shot this was. *They don't owe me any favors, and we aren't technically even friends. I'm sure they'll say no.*

"Well, here we are," Nick said with his signature smirk.

"Can I ask a huge favor of you guys?" I said, ignoring Nick's response. I reached to fiddle with my bracelet, and when I remembered it was gone, slid my hand down to my fingers.

"Sure, what is it?" Justin said, answering for all of them.

"Well, the thing is, the showcase my family is helping with—their entertainment in the middle of the dance category can't make it. I was wondering if you guys would be willing to perform?" I managed to get it out without fumbling over my words and only talking slightly too fast.

I could tell they were all taking a moment to think it over. I continued fiddling with my fingers while studying their faces. I couldn't read Justin's expression, but I could see the gears in his head turning. Nick had a glint of excitement in his eye to go along with his signature smirk. Adam and Tommy slowly grew smiles on their face.

Tommy was the first to say anything. "That's fine with me, but it has to be okay with all of us," he said, looking around at the others for a response.

I nodded my head.

"Sure. It's not like we're really busy anyhow," Nick said nonchalantly.

"Sounds fun, and the more publicity, the better. I'm up for it," Adam said, adding his opinion.

Justin. That just leaves Justin. He is the last person I need to say yes. I looked at him in anticipation of his answer. *He can make or break this.*

"Okay, we'll perform," he said with an even tone. I let out a relieved breath, but Justin continued, "On one condition."

Chapter 15

Condition! What on Earth could he want? Why does he have to have a condition? I have no idea what his condition is, but I am willing to do anything to help the showcase. The showcase is important to my family, and what matters to them matters to me. Not to mention it would feel good to know I was able to contribute to something bigger than myself for once.

"Okay, what's the condition?" I asked hesitantly.

"I've run into Incognito Moves around the hotel a couple of times, and I think it would be cool if she would perform with us," Justin said.

My brain hit a brick wall, and my entire body stood on edge. It seemed like he was implying something by making the condition to me about Incognito. *Does he know?* I'm sure I looked like a deer caught in the headlights for a minute. I couldn't form any words. I was caught completely off guard. I finally got my gears to start spinning and words to come out.

"Who is Incognito Moves?" I asked, furrowing my eyebrow and trying my best to act confused. To my surprise, Tommy, not Justin, was the one to answer my question.

"She's a super talented YouTube dancer who wears a mask when she dances to conceal her identity."

My mind was in overdrive looking for a way out of Justin's condition.

"Okay...That's great and all that you want to perform with this YouTuber, but how are you expecting I contact her? She may be at the hotel, but I don't even know who she is. Let's say I do happen to find her. What do I ask? 'Hey, I don't know you, but will you do me a favor and perform in a showcase?'" I crossed my arms, challenging Justin's condition.

I was trying to see if Justin knew I was her or not. "I'm not expecting you to find her. I'll find her and ask her myself. If I can get her to say yes, we'll do it," Justin said with confidence.

The guys looked at me for my response. I was hesitant. "Well...I mean if you can talk to this Incognito person and get her to say yes, then the showcase will agree to have you both."

Justin smiled victoriously.

"That's great and all, but how do you plan to find her, Justin?" Nick asked in confusion.

"I have my ways. You guys stay here. She's not real big on meeting new people, so I don't want to overwhelm her. I'll go find her and tell you guys what she says," Justin said as he left the room.

I stayed in the room long enough for them not to be suspicious and then said, "I'm going to go update the head of the showcase so she knows what's going on."

I hurried to my room with my thoughts reeling. Updating Rachel was the least of my worries. *Why on Earth does Justin have to ask Incognito Moves to dance with them? How does he even think he'll find her? Wait, what makes him think she'll say yes? What, with just two encounters, he thinks they're best friends!?*

Maybe he knows I'm Incognito. No, he couldn't. My parents haven't even figured it out. I shook all the thoughts out of my head. *Okay, first I need to calm down. I need to decide if I want to dance with them or not. I mean, it's good exposure; but since when do I care about exposure? It's not like Advanced Company would figure out who she was, but maybe they would. I've never performed live. It would be a new experience, but I have stage fright.*

I was mildly panicking inside. Okay, mildly was a lie; I was majorly freaking out. I grabbed my bag with my dance stuff and sped to the conference wing bathroom to change—like all the other times. I walked out already in my mask in case Justin was around. I figured if he was looking for Incognito, this wing is where he would be.

I entered the room I usually danced in to find Justin waiting there. I stopped dead in my tracks when I saw him. When he heard the door open, he looked up to see who it was.

"Hey," was all he said.

"So, you're stalking me now?" I asked, doing my best to add playfulness to my tone. Justin chuckled at my comment.

"No, I needed to ask a favor of you," he said, getting straight to business. Justin crossed from the other side of the room to where I was standing.

I countered by walking past him into the room to drop my bag down while saying, "Why on Earth do you think I would do a favor for you? We aren't exactly friends." *Ouch. That was a little harsh. Okay, that was extremely harsh. I need better people skills.*

"Why don't you hear me out before you shoot me down like that?" he asked.

If Justin was irritated or hurt by my response, he didn't show it. He kept his composure.

"What exactly is it that you need my help for?" I asked, softening my tone. Justin took a deep breath before saying,

"My dance group, Advanced Company, and I we were asked to perform today at a showcase that's going on here." He paused for a moment.

"What's this got to do with me?" I asked, trying my best to lace confusion in my tone since he couldn't see my face.

"Well, we—or, well, I—gave them one condition…" he said, rubbing the back of his neck. Whether this was out of embarrassment or nervousness, I wasn't sure. Justin then continued, "that you had to dance with us for us to say yes to the showcase." Justin finished and stood awkwardly waiting for my response.

Not knowing what to say, I answered with a question, "Why?" He stood there a minute with confusion written all over his face. "Why am I the condition?" I asked, clarifying my question.

"Well, to be honest, I thought it may be my group's only chance to dance with you. You're an extremely talented dancer. It's a once-in-a-lifetime opportunity. Besides, you deserve the experience of performing in front of a live audience," he reasoned.

I mentally laughed. *Performing with me is a once-in-a-lifetime opportunity?* That's a bit of a stretch.

When he could tell I wasn't going to agree immediately, he continued. "It's helping a good friend of mine. It gets you exposure and shows everyone what a great dancer you are. Plus, if I'm honest, I just want an excuse to dance with Incognito Moves." At the last statement, I saw his cheeks flare with pink. He was more than a little embarrassed.

Even though I already knew Justin was going to ask this, I still didn't have an answer for him. *I'm still not sure if I want to do it. It's risky. I've never performed in front of a live audience before. That could be fun…or terrifying. No one has ever wanted to collaborate with me—or well, Incognito—before.*

I sighed. "I don't know," was all I managed to say as I diverted my gaze from Justin's. I was afraid to perform, but I was also afraid that if I didn't say yes, they wouldn't dance in the showcase. Then Rachel wouldn't have an act to inspire the new dancers. *I have the chance to help someone, to do something good. Would it make me a bad person if I could save the showcase and I just stood by and did nothing? What would someone else do in this situation?*

"Please, it would be so much fun. I promise this is not to figure out who you are. My crew and I just want a chance to perform with you. You're an awesome dancer, and we think it would be fun. Plus, it would give you a chance to get over your stage fright," he said persuasively. My head snapped back toward Justin at his statement.

"Wait, stage fright? What makes you think I have stage fright?" I asked, offended. More accurately, I was shocked that he pegged me that well.

Justin was quick to say, "Well, it's kind of apparent, or at least I think it is. You wear a mask to hide your identity; that way people don't know it's you. By doing that, if you get criticism, it's not personal. Also, if when I saw you dance the first time is any indication, you don't like people watching you dance. Hence the conclusion: stage fright."

I couldn't believe what I was hearing. *He thinks he has me figured out, when he barely knows me. Yes, I have stage fright, but that's not the only reason I wear the mask—or is it? I mean, it certainly helps, but it's more than that, right? The mask isn't just something to hide behind. It has a purpose.* I realized I was no longer sure why I did anything I did.

"You're quite perceptive, aren't you?" I paused for a brief moment before continuing. "You may be partially right. I don't like to perform in front of live audiences. That is part of why I wear the mask, but it's not the only reason."

"What are your other reasons?" Justin asked, genuinely intrigued.

I wasn't expecting him to ask that. Okay, I was expecting him to ask that, but I was optimistic that he wouldn't.

"That's for another time. There is a little bit more pressing matter to finish discussing," I said, diverting the conversation.

Justin nodded in agreement. "I agree, so what's your answer?"

I don't know what came over me—if it was a moment of weakness, great courage, or sheer stupidity. Maybe it was the pleading and hopeful look on his face? I don't know what caused it, but I said the one word I had tried to keep myself from saying the entire time.

Chapter 16

"Yes. I'll perform with you guys." My answer made Justin's face light up like a Christmas tree. His shock and excitement were obvious.

"That's great! Do you want to come with me to tell the guys, or do you just want to stay here, and I'll bring them back in a few?"

I thought of the best course of action. "Bring them back in 30 minutes. I have to go do something real quickly," I said.

"Awesome! Thank you so much. You won't regret this," he said, leaving the room.

It's a little late for regret. What did I get myself into?

I waited a few minutes before changing and heading to the teen lounge. The guys had been waiting for me to get back before Justin shared the news.

"Hey, Rachel the event coordinator told me to tell her what the final decision was," I said, covering up for my earlier departure. I felt guilty for lying.

"Well," Justin started off, " I got her to say yes. Incognito Moves is dancing with us. We meet her in one of the conference rooms in about 20 minutes." A series of high-fives erupted, the excitement evident by all of their beaming faces. They all started to talk at once.

"What if we get to see who she is?"

"What if we get her phone number or—"

Justin cut everyone off. "I did promise her that this wasn't about finding out who she was. This is strictly professional for us, okay, guys?" The rest of them nodded in understanding.

"Okay, now the performance is at 4:15, and you guys need to create a routine with her," I said, reminding them that they weren't in smooth water yet.

"We are going to go meet up with her now, and I'm assuming we'll just start then," Justin said.

"Okay, I'll go let Rachel know you guys agreed," I said before leaving the room and quickly rushing to find a quiet spot where I could call Rachael and update her.

I came across an empty conference room and figured it was as good a spot as any. I slid my phone out of my pocket and dialed Racheal with my stomach in knots. *What is she going to think about Justin's condition?*

I heard Rachel's voice come over the phone. "Hello?"

"Rachel? It's Kinsley," I said.

"Hey Kinsley. Any update on the dance group?" she asked.

"I got the group to say yes, but they had one condition," I said fiddling with my hands. There was a pause before Rachel spoke.

"What was the condition?" Her voice was full of skepticism.

"They wanted another dancer who goes by Incognito Moves to perform with them. She's a dancer with a big following online."

"If that's what it takes. I don't have any other options right now. If you guys can get her, that's fine with me."

I let out a mental sigh of relief.

"She already said yes, and Advanced Company said yes as well."

"That's great! Thank you!" she said gratefully.

"No problem; do they need to have an on-stage rehearsal or anything?" I asked, trying to get all the details.

"I'll just need the song selection ahead of time, and they need to be backstage by 3:45. That's it. This is all so last minute that it's not possible to have a run-through on stage," she said, thinking everything through.

"Okay, I'll be sure to let them know."

"Great! I'll talk to you later," Rachel said before hanging up.

I let out a heavy sigh of relief. *I can't believe she agreed to this. Now to go hunt down Advanced Company.*

To my luck, I ran into them in the hall.

"I just finished talking to Rachel, the director of the showcase, and all she needs from you guys is song selection and to be backstage by 3:45. There's no time for a run-through on stage," I said, filling them in.

"That's not a problem. Once we talk to Incognito, we'll get you our song selection," Justin said.

"Okay great. I'll see you in a little bit," I said before walking off.

I burst into the bathroom and changed into my dance clothes and mask. I hurried out and into the room I danced in. Sure enough, they were already waiting.

"Hey," I said, ending at the door. The guys politely greeted her (me).

"This is the rest of Advanced Company," Justin said. He then began pointing to each member. "This is Adam, Tommy, and Nick."

"Nice to meet you all," I said.

"Well, we have a full routine to choreograph. Do you just want to dance in here?" Justin asked.

"That's fine," I said, trying to keep my talking to a minimum in hopes that they wouldn't figure out who I was.

"How do we go about this? We only have five hours to create an entire routine. We usually have days," Adam said, bringing everyone to the realization that this was not an easy task.

Adam was right. We didn't have time to choreograph a brand new routine. Well, not a good one anyhow.

"Adam's right. I'm not sure how we pull this off," Nick said in exasperation. I racked my brain for an answer to our problem but came up empty-handed.

"I agree. We can't create a whole new routine in that amount of time. However, we can just tweak an existing routine," Justin said.

I shot Justin a confused look but then realized my mask was on, so he wouldn't be able to see my reaction. Facial expressions wouldn't cut it. I was going to have to voice everything I was thinking.

"That's great for you guys, but I don't know your routines," I said, pointing out the one major flaw in his idea.

"We can teach you, and anything that's too hard to remember or out of your comfort zone, we can change. You can put your own flare on the dance," Justin said. When I didn't respond, he added, "Besides, I would put money on you being a fast learner."

I shifted my sights to the wall as I considered his proposal. *It would be quicker than creating a new dance from scratch. However, I'm the only one who has to learn anything new. I could mess the entire thing up.*

"We don't really have a choice," Adam declared, rationalizing the situation. I let out a heavy sigh.

"Then what are we waiting for?" I asked, trying to summon all my courage.

Justin gave me a warm smile before shifting his attention to the boys. "What about the routine we performed for the show we just did?"

"That's a great idea," Nick said enthusiastically. The boys began teaching me the routine step by step. Just as I mentally predicted, I started out as a full-on train wreck. I couldn't get any of the moves right. It took me forever to learn just a couple simple combinations. My frustration slowly built, until I was so mad at myself I was ready to explode.

"Let's take five," Justin suggested, noticing my frustration.

I hurried out to the hall and slumped against the wall. I shoved a hand through my hair. I couldn't take this—mess-up after mess-up. The guys didn't seem to care. They were all being nice about it. I was the one who was mad at myself. I slid my back down the wall until I was sitting with my knees bent. I leaned my head against the wall and closed my eyes. *Could this get any worse?*

Just then, the door to the rehearsal room opened. The answer to that question? Yes. Yes, it just got worse. I didn't bother to look at who had come out, but I knew I wanted to be alone. All of a sudden, I felt the presence of someone sitting next to me. *Great, this person has decided to stay.*

We sat in silence for a moment until the mystery person spoke. "Are you okay?"

I gave a curt laugh. *Yes, I'm clearly doing great.*

The no-longer mystery man, Justin, was quick to apologize. "Sorry. I don't know why I asked that. You're obviously frustrated."

"Of course I'm frustrated. I'm messing up simple combinations. At this rate, I'll never get the routine," I said exasperatedly.

"They aren't that simple." All I did to respond was turn my head and glare at him from under my mask. Somehow he could sense the emotion in my face without seeing it. "Okay, they are simple, but you're nervous. I get it. You're not used to performing live," Justin empathized.

"That's not an excuse," I remarked, looking down at my lap.

"I wasn't making excuses for you," he said, making a point.

Justin's voice softened, "I was saying *I get it*." He let that settle in the air for a moment before continuing. "The problem isn't that you can't get the moves. You have each move down perfectly. The problem is you're so focused on making each motion perfect that you're rigid. You aren't smooth in transitioning between moves. You need to let the dance flow." I took in everything Justin had said.

I didn't want to admit it, but he was right. I was thinking too much. I wasn't allowing myself to ease into the next move.

"When did you become so wise?" I asked. Justin chuckled.

"I'm not wise. I've been where you are. I use to be the slowest in the group with learning new choreography," Justin stated.

"I doubt that," I said in disbelief.

"It's true," Justin responded while standing up. Justin extended his hand to help me up. "Ready to try again?" I grabbed Justin's hand and allowed him to pull me to my feet.

"What are we waiting for?" I answered with a newfound courage.

"Break's over," Justin announced upon returning to the room. The boys all stood up, and we began working on the choreography again. I attempted the first combination of moves and instantly recognized what Justin had said about being rigid. I took a deep breath and tried the moves again—this time, allowing the moves to flow. Justin gave me a knowing smile, once I completed the moves with ease.

I was back. From then on, learning the rest of the dance went more quickly than expected. It helped that I already had watched Advanced Company rehearse and perform it. The boys allowed me to add or change the routine wherever I felt necessary. I finished learning the last combination, and then Justin announced it was time to run it with music.

Once the music started, we began our dance. I messed up a few times, but overall, it wasn't horrible. As soon as the dance finished, I said, "Let's go again." I knew that I needed more practice to internalize it into my body. No one objected. We ran the dance until all of the rough patches were smoothed out, and everyone felt confident about it.

I looked at the clock, and to my surprise, it was only 2:50 p.m.

"I'd say that's a wrap," I remarked with excitement.

"I believe it is," Nick said in agreement.

"What else do we have to do?" I asked, knowing all too well there wasn't anything else required of us.

"All that's left is to be backstage by 3:45," Justin replied.

"Great, then I'll meet you guys there," I said as I strode over to my bag and began packing up my stuff.

"Should we try and coordinate our outfits?" Nick asked as an afterthought.

"That's up to you guys," I spoke as I slung my bag over my shoulder.

"Why don't we just try and match in color?" Tommy suggested.

"That will work; how about blue and black?" I asked, knowing that would be easy to find in the stuff I brought.

"I like that," Adam said.

"Then it's settled. I'll see you all backstage, dressed in blue and black, at 3:45," I called over my shoulder on my way out the door.

Chapter 17

Back in my room, I tossed the clothes I planned to wear during the performance into my bag and headed back to the conference wing. I pulled my phone out of my pocket and texted Rachel. I told her the song, the name of Advanced Company, the name of Incognito Moves, and a slight description of Advanced Company and Incognito. I instantly got a text back with a simple "thank you."

I decided to stay around the showcase wing until it was time to perform. I found a bench near the wing and sat down to listen to music for a while—and be alone with my thoughts. I had my eyes closed, just enjoying the music and trying to calm my nerves, when I felt the presence of someone else on the bench next to me.

I opened my eyes to see who had sat down next to me. I was not surprised to see Justin. *So much for being alone with my thoughts*, I reflected yet again. I took my headphones out and paused my music.

"Hey," he said.

"Hey, what are you doing here?" I asked.

"Looking for you, of course."

"Oh really?" I gave him a skeptical look, not believing him at all. He chuckled at my reaction.

"Is it so hard to believe that I enjoy your company?" he said. My mind hit a brick wall. I was expecting a joking response in return, not that. Before I responded he continued, "That, and I also needed to give you our song selection."

"Oh, right, what did you decide on?" I inquired, even though I already knew the answer.

Justin explained to me how they didn't have a lot of time, so they came to the conclusion that it would be best to use an old routine. He told me they decided just to tweak the one they had done for their show.

It's weird having someone explain a series of events to you like you had no idea what happened when you were there, I thought to myself.

"I'll make sure to get Rachel the song," I said, knowing full well I already had told her. I glanced down at the phone in my hand and considered asking Justin for his phone number. The thought made me nervous. *It would be a weird thing to ask. I hardly know him. But if I got his phone number, I could stay in contact with Advanced Company even once they left the hotel...*

Just then, my phone sounded before I could make a decision. I opened the text from my dad: "Where are you? The acting portion has started, and Ty performs next."

"Oh shoot, I forgot my little brother has his acting thing today, and I am supposed to watch. I have to go," I said, quickly standing up.

Justin stood up with me. "I'll come with you; it sounds interesting."

I didn't have time to argue with him or question why he wanted to come. "Sure, but I hope you're willing to run, because otherwise I'll miss his performance," I stated before sprinting to the showcase with Justin in tow. I burst through the doors right as they had finished introducing my brother. He came out on stage, gave an encouraging short speech, and started the monologue he had prepared.

I couldn't help but think about what a great actor he was, especially for his age. I always wished I had talent like his—and the guts to get up in front of people and perform with ease. My thoughts wandered. *He was made for the spotlight. Ty has a personality that just draws people to him. I, on the other hand, was designed for behind the scenes. When my brother acts, it's like the whole room is in a trance. You can't divert your attention, for fear that you'll miss something.*

He finished, and I told Justin to follow me, making my way back to where my brother would be. I knocked on the door to the small room for returning performances to get staged in, and Ty opened it. Before I could even congratulate him, he engulfed me in a hug.

"Did you see me? How did I do?" he asked with a hint of nervousness. I couldn't help but smile at his energy and nerves.

"You did absolutely amazingly!" I marveled, giving him the biggest smile I could.

He beamed back at me. "Thanks!" Just then he noticed Justin, "Who's he?" Ty asked with curiosity and a smile.

"I'm friends with your sister. My group and I are going to perform during the dance portion," Justin said, answering Ty's question before I could.

There's that word "friend" again. He's barely known me for a few days, and he already considers me a friend. I don't know what to think about that.

"Oh cool! I'm sure you know then that Kinsley loves to dance," Ty announced. I mentally cringed at Ty bringing up the topic of dance.

"No, I didn't know that. You must be holding out on me, Kinsley," Justin said with a mischievous grin.

"All right, he probably has to get going. I'll see you later, Ty—and again, great job!" I said as Justin and I left the room.

"Your brother's great," Justin stated randomly.

I smiled at his sudden comment. "That's one word for him."

Justin chuckled at my response. "I still have time to kill before the performance, what do you want to do?"

I looked at the time. "You don't have much time left. It's 3:30."

"Oh yeah, I have to go. Are you going to be at the performance?" he asked hopefully.

"Of course," *whether I like it or not.*

We both said bye, and he left. I hoofed it to the bathroom again and changed into my performance outfit. I wore black pants, a light-blue short-sleeved shirt, and light-blue sneakers. I looked in the mirror and took a deep breath before slipping on my mask. I emerged from the bathroom and took off toward backstage.

I can't believe I was talked into this.

I was the first one to make it backstage. As I was waiting, I couldn't help but think about what a bad idea this was.

I'm not sure I'm going to make it through the performance. What if I forget the moves or return to being rigid, or my mask falls off? Or…

Before I could finish my string of thoughts, the guys approached. They all wore entirely different outfits, but each matched by wearing black and some shade of blue.

"You ready?" Justin asked.

"Yep," I stammered, struggling to keep my voice from shaking.

The real answer to that question is no, not in a million years will I be ready to dance in front of this many people. I'm petrified. This is my first time performing live, and they've performed live hundreds of times. I know I'm going to mess up somehow. I am the amateur amongst soon to be pros.

"Don't worry; you'll do great," Justin said, clearly trying to help my nerves.

"Is it that obvious?" I asked, glad that I had my mask on, as I felt the heat rise on my cheeks.

"Not to the other guys. I'm just perceptive. You've been fiddling with your hands the entire time," Justin said, pointing at my hands and explaining how he knew.

I glanced over and saw the other guys were oblivious, just talking amongst themselves. Justin continued, "Don't be nervous; you're a great dancer. Just imagine you're in front of your camera." I nodded my head and tried to calm myself down. "Don't forget, you're performing with a group. You're not alone out there. If something goes wrong, we've got your back," Justin added, putting a reassuring hand on my shoulder.

A hidden smile slowly formed under my mask. "Thanks," I said. My nerves hadn't settled completely, but it was comforting to know there were other people out on stage with me.

I then heard the MC start to introduce us: "Now we have a very special treat for you. We have Advanced Company teaming up with a popular new YouTuber, performing live for her very first time. Some of you may have heard of her: Incognito Moves!" The MC left the stage, and we made our way to our starting positions.

The music blared from the speakers, and my nerves washed away, as I focused all my energy on dancing the routine and feeling the music. All I did was dance and let my worries fade away. It was energizing with all the people there. All my pent-up nerves felt like electricity shooting through my body. The experience felt completely different than when I danced in front of my camera, but it was a good different.

We executed the routine flawlessly. We finished, and everyone cheered loudly. The audience clearly loved our performance. We exited the stage and gave each other high-fives. Happiness flooded over me. *I performed live for the first time, and I didn't screw it up.*

"That was amazing!" I chimed. I could feel the adrenaline pumping through my veins. It was like I was on cloud nine.

My heart was racing as fast as a bullet train. It was like I could feel the energy pumping through my body.

"What did I tell you? I knew you would do great!" Justin shot me a cheeky grin.

"I guess you were right this once," I remarked, with my mask hiding my smile.

"Thanks for performing with us," Adam said.

"You're welcome. It was a lot of fun," I said honestly. "Well, I should get going. " They all said goodbye as I left. I returned to the bathroom to change back into normal clothes before starting the voyage upstairs, all the while smiling ear to ear. *I just performed live, and I killed it.*

Chapter 18

As I approached the elevator, I spotted Ty and Darren there waiting.

"Hey guys, where's Mom and Dad?" I asked once I reached them.

"They had just a couple more things they had to do at the showcase before they could leave," Darren explained. I just nodded. I took out my iPhone and checked the time. It was only 4:35 p.m.

"Hey guys, since it's only 4:35, do you want to go hit the water park?" I inquired.

Immediately, Ty's face lit up. "Yes!" he nearly shouted.

"Eh, why not?" Darren said, much less enthusiastically than Ty.

Back in the hotel room, we all changed into our swimsuits and grabbed towels.

"I'm going to leave a note for Mom and Dad, so they know where we went." The boys waited for me to finish writing.

In the elevator, I noticed that Ty couldn't sit still. He was practically bouncing up and down. I just grinned at his boyish energy. We reached the indoor water park and picked a set of chairs upon which to set our stuff down.

"Where to first?" Darren asked.

Ty instantly responded, "I want to do that slide." I followed his hand to where it pointed, and I saw a bright yellow body slide. Darren and I had no objections, so we all walked over to the slide. Well, Ty more speed-walked/ran, and Darren and I just walked. Much to my enjoyment, the line wasn't long. The closer we got to the top of the slide, the more Ty's excitement built.

When it was almost our turn, we saw there were three different slides to choose from. Darren and I gave each other a knowing look.

"We should race," Darren said, dawning a smug grin.

"Why the smug look? You think you're gonna win, don't you?" I questioned skeptically. Darren gave me a *duh* look and said, "We both know I always win."

I rolled my eyes. "We'll just see about that," I said with a challenging tone.

We all sat in our separate slides, waiting for the lifeguard to give us the go ahead. As soon as he said it was safe to go, I propelled myself forward with my arms. I was in a tube slide, so I was soon in complete darkness. The sound of the rushing water mixed with the faint babble of voices. It was peaceful just listening to the sound of rushing water, not thinking about anything else.

Within what felt like a few seconds, I saw the light at the end of the tube and knew the slide was about to end. I flushed out into the water and saw Darren had just exited his slide moments before me. As I turned my head to the other slide, I saw Ty come out right after me.

Ty and I waded through the pool to Darren. "Looks like you won," I congratulated him.

"Yeah, I knew I would win, because I'm just that awesome," Darren said, crossing his arms with a cocky smile. I rolled my eyes at his fake cockiness. I knew Darren wasn't as cocky as he came across. He was only that way around Ty and me, and even then it was just in a joking way.

I looked over at an oddly quiet Ty and noticed he was quite upset, probably over losing the race. "Ty, you choose the next slide," I said, hoping to divert his attention elsewhere.

He instantly perked up. "Okay!"

"Where do you want to go?" I asked.

Ty thought for a while as he looked around at all the different slides. "Let's do that one." My eyes followed his gaze, and I saw it was one of the slides with the huge inner tubes that typically sat six or eight people. I loved those slides. They were a lot of fun, since they involved riding with other people rather than alone. You got to watch the expression of others as you went down the slide.

There's something about sharing a fun moment with other people instead of being isolated. At least that's what I think.

We navigated our way to the slide. Unfortunately, that line was super long; but the time quickly passed as we talked and joked back and forth. We reached the top, and I noticed the inner tube was a six-seater. That meant we would probably have two or three other people with us. We got in the inner tube, and the lifeguard directed three other people to ride with us.

The lifeguard pushed the inner tube slightly to give it momentum, and off we went, plummeting down the slide. Throughout the whole slide, Ty whooped and hollered—and Darren, of course, ended up joining in.

I just smiled at my brother's goofiness. The boys even had the other people who rode with us laughing. I was happy as I watched this scene unfold. I knew it was such a regular thing that wasn't that extravagant, but it would be a cherished memory for me: just the three of us hanging out and enjoying life.

We don't get a lot of these moments, I thought to myself. Often their goofball ways were part of what made them so annoying, but I realized I still wouldn't want them any other way.

Once at the bottom of the slide, we climbed out of the inner tube and trudged through the splash pool until we were on dry ground. Ty proceeded to yell, "That was awesome!" I laughed at my brother's enthusiasm and looked over to find even Darren smiling ear to ear. I had to admit, it was a fun slide. The fun was amplified by being with my brothers.

"Where to next?" Ty asked, bouncing up and down on his toes.

We stood there a minute until we agreed upon what slide to do next. We hung around the water park for a while, doing any and every slide imaginable, racing when we could and laughing a lot.

We got back to our stuff, where I checked the time and saw it was 8:30 p.m. I couldn't believe we had been there for so long. *I guess it's true: time flies when you're having fun,* I thought.

"We should probably head up," Darren said.

I nodded in agreement. "Definitely." We grabbed our stuff. On our way up to the room, Ty wouldn't stop talking about the fun experience and which slides he preferred.

It was impossible not to smile at Ty's excitement. Darren was even cracking a smile at how much Ty was beaming.

Back in the room, we stepped inside to find Mom and Dad sitting on the couch.

"Hey, guys! How was the water park?" Dad asked.

Ty was the first to answer, no surprise there, "It was amazing!"

Mom and Dad smiled at his joy. "That's great to hear," Mom said.

I smiled. "I'm gonna go change. I'll be right back," I said as I departed to my room.

I hurriedly changed out of my swimsuit. Back in the family room, I found Darren and Ty had also changed and joined my parents. I took a seat in the only open chair.

"Who's hungry?" Dad asked.

Darren and Ty responded with a resounding, "Me!"

"Yeah, I could eat," I said, shrugging. I hadn't realized I was hungry, but now that it was mentioned, I realized I wouldn't mind a meal.

"All right, let's head out then and find some food," Mom said. We all got up and ventured out of the hotel for the first time in our vacation—in search of someplace good to eat.

Chapter 19

We didn't take long to choose a restaurant that we all thought sounded good. Once we were all inside and had ordered, everyone started talking about their day. Ty raved about how awesome his had been. He recalled everything from performing his monologue to how incredible the water park was. Even Darren shared how great his day had turned out to be.

I started to think through my day. What I believed was going to be a non-eventful, dull day was instead quite exciting and full of new experiences. For the first time, I'd danced in front of a live audience, which was both fantastic and terrifying. It was also my first time dancing with a group, which was a nice change.

I was pulled from my thoughts by my mom asking me a question that I didn't quite hear, because I was lost in thought. "I'm sorry, what was that?" I asked.

"I said, how was your day?" she said, repeating herself.

"Oh, it was great. A lot of fun," I replied with a genuine smile.

"Did you get to see the professional dancers who performed? I know how much you love to dance," Dad said.

I nodded, "Yeah, I was there. The dance group is pretty well known. The YouTuber, on the other hand, is kind of new," I shared, as though it was nothing special.

"The YouTuber was really good," Ty said. I didn't say anything in response.

"Yes, she was quite impressive," Mom said, agreeing with Ty.

I was smiling inwardly. I had no idea my family had seen me dance. It was weird to receive praise from my family, when they had no idea they were complimenting me.

I knew it was wrong to be keeping a secret from my family. I just hadn't gotten around to telling them. They were always busy. I didn't figure they had time to be bothered with such a non-eventful thing. Plus, I didn't feel it mattered. I was just a YouTuber, and there were plenty of other talented dancers on YouTube, I told myself.

I was also afraid that on the off chance my parents would take an interest in it, they would be convinced that I should reveal who I was or become a professional dancer. I wasn't ready for either of those things.

I can't deal with the pressure of living up to being a professional. That would open the door for more criticism. People would expect more from me. Not to mention the worry of letting my parents down. I already struggle enough with keeping my parents happy; I don't need another area of my life where I'm walking on eggshells. I need my mom to be just that: a mom, not a manager.

Mom brought me out of my thoughts again. "Sweetie, tomorrow's the masquerade that the showcase is holding, and since you didn't bring a dress, I thought we could go dress shopping tomorrow." Mom's eyes sparkled with excitement.

"Oh… you see. The thing is…" there was no good way to say this, "I hadn't really planned on going." I blurted the last part out a little too quickly.

Despite my speed, I could tell Mom heard every word, because the sparkle in her eye disappeared and her smile fell.

"What do you mean you're not going?" The disappointment was written all over her face.

"Well, I didn't figure it would matter if I went or not. I wasn't part of the showcase. Actually, I wasn't even sure if I was allowed to go. I also don't understand why they're having a masquerade. It doesn't make any sense."

"Of course you're allowed to go. It's for the families of contestants as well as the actual contestants. It gives a chance for agents and managers to talk to some of the contestants, and it's a way for the showcase to thank everyone for being a part of it," Mom said, as though she were spelling something out. Mom continued, "I promise it will be a lot of fun."

I saw how hopeful my mom was, and I finally caved. I did not want to disappoint her. "Okay, fine I'll go," I said reluctantly.

"Yes! I promise you won't regret it. You and I can get breakfast in the morning and then go find a dress for you; sound good?" Her previous sparkle had returned.

"Yeah, that sounds good," I answered.

The rest of dinner, I stayed quiet for the most part—only commenting here and there. Once we finished, we headed back to the hotel. We all watched something on TV together. Mom was the first to go to bed—and then Dad. My brothers soon followed. I went to my room, grabbed my bag, slipped my dance stuff in it, and headed out.

I strolled to the showcase wing and changed in the bathroom as usual—before entering the room I typically danced in. Tonight, I wasn't filming. I was just dancing for fun. I planned to try out some new stuff. However, I still put my mask on, in case someone were to stumble across me dancing.

I had just finished trying a new trick when I heard the door shut. I turned around and found none other than Justin. *Surprise, surprise.*

"To what do I owe this pleasure?" I said with a slight smile, even though he couldn't see it under my mask.

"Oh, you know. Just wanted to see your pretty face," he said.

Wait; did he just call me pretty? Oh, the mask. It was a joke.

He continued after a short pause, "I thought I would drop by to thank you."

I was more than a little surprised and confused. "Thank me for what?" I asked.

"Yeah, thank you for performing with us. I know it was uncomfortable for you. I—or we—all really appreciated and enjoyed it," Justin said.

I found myself being honest with my response. "You know, at first it was really uncomfortable. However, it was a nice change to dance with a group."

He smiled at my response. "Good. I'm glad."

Silence filled the air. Justin rubbed the back of his neck and then continued. "I'm probably overstepping, but would you mind having someone else to dance with right now? If you don't want me to, that's cool too. I'll find a different room."

It seems our roles are reversed for once: I'm not the one feeling uncomfortable. When did that happen? I thought briefly before responding, not giving my answer a second thought.

"Sure. I would love to have someone else to pass ideas back and forth," I said with a cheerful tone.

Justin smiled at my answer and shrugged off his jacket. We decided to look through songs until we found one that we agreed on. We decided to style the song more towards contemporary.

As we choreographed the song and I saw him easily pick up the moves, I realized how diverse in dance Justin was. Before then, I had only seen him dance hip hop. But we were doing contemporary, and he executed it flawlessly—and created more than half the choreography. I was amazed at his skill—and quite shocked.

Though I'm not sure why I would be surprised, I told myself. *I barely know him. I'm sure there's a lot of things I don't know about him.*

We worked our way through the choreography pretty quickly until we got to the end, where we struggled to find a fitting way to close the dance. We threw ideas back and forth, finally coming up with something cool we both liked.

"You ready to run it from the top?" Justin asked.

"I was born ready," I said with confidence.

"Okay, then let's see what damage we can do," he said, clapping his hands together.

I walked over and turned on the music. It felt natural to dance with Justin. We flawlessly moved in-sync. I had never danced with a partner before. It felt strange.

There's an unspoken trust between partners. A connection. The idea that you're not alone; there's another person to lean on. Someone who gets you. Someone who has your back.

As different as it was, I enjoyed every step. The song ended, and Justin held both his hands up for a double high-five.

"That was pretty amazing, if I do say so myself!" Justin beamed.

"I would have to agree with you there. We make a pretty good team. It was a nice change getting to dance with some-one else," I said.

"We do make a good team. Have you ever danced with a partner before?" he inquired curiously.

"Nope, before the performance with you guys, I hadn't danced with a group either. A day of firsts, I guess." I paused, considering whether I wanted to continue or not.

I let my curiosity get the best of me, and I asked, "What about you? Do you work with a partner often?"

"Well, obviously I'm used to working with a group, and I do work with a partner pretty often. At my dance studio back home, I do multiple styles of dance. Quite a few of them involve partners. Do you go to a dance studio?"

"No, I don't. Everything I've learned is self-taught," I said.

Justin's eyes slightly widened. "That's impressive."

I glanced at the clock on the wall and saw it was 11:30 p.m. "It's getting late; I should go," I said, gathering my bag.

"Yeah, I should probably get back to my room too," he replied in agreement. "If the rest of the group woke up, I'm sure they'd be wondering where I am. I enjoyed getting to dance with you."

"You too; it was fun," I said, slinging my bag over my shoulder.

We both left to the hall, and I turned the lights out in the room on our way out. For a minute, we stood in silence. Surprisingly, it wasn't awkward. I think we both didn't know what to say. Unsurprisingly, Justin was the first to speak up.

"Well, I'll see you around. Hopefully, we can dance again sometime," he said. I could see the hopefulness in his eyes.

"Yeah, hopefully," was all I could bring myself to say.

Justin walked off to return to his room. I stood there a minute, giving him a head start so I wouldn't risk running into him again. I started the route to my room—mask and all—knowing that no one would be around this late.

I arrived at the door of my family's room, took off my mask, and slipped it in my bag on the off chance someone would be awake. I quietly went to my room. I got ready for bed, turned out my light, and laid down.

As I lay in bed, it suddenly dawned on me that I had to go dress shopping the next morning. I let out a light groan.

I closed my eyes and willed sleep to come, but I just lay there awake. My head was reeling from the day's events. I couldn't get over the fact that with some help, I'd overcome my stage fright. I realized Justin was a crucial part of that.

That's the way Justin is; he looks out for his friends. Friend. I smiled at the thought that four complete strangers had become my friends in a handful of days. *I guess time doesn't always determine friendship.*

Chapter 20

I woke the next day, surprisingly feeling refreshed, despite taking a while to fall asleep the night before. I got out of bed, remembered I had to go dress shopping, and sighed.

I don't want to go to the dumb masquerade anyway, let alone take the time out of my day to get a dress for it. On the bright side, I get to spend some one-on-one time with my mom, and that is a rare occurrence.

That alone was worth the torture of going to the masquerade. I got dressed and ready for the day, headed out into the kitchen, and poured a glass of water.

I was the only one out of their room. I hunkered down on the couch and went on my phone. Shortly, I heard my parents' door open. Mom sauntered out, dressed and ready to face the day.

She smiled when she saw me. "Ready?" she asked, too chipper for it being so early.

"Yep." However, if I were answering truthfully, my answer would have been, *nope.*

Mom grabbed the rental car keys, and we exited the room. As we walked through the lobby, I saw the members of Advanced Company just getting to the dining area. Adam noticed me and waved. I gave a smile and quick wave back as we walked by. The others turned to see who Adam had waved at, and when the rest of them saw me, we exchanged waves.

My mom, not missing a beat, questioned, "Aren't they that dance group from the other day?"

"Yeah, that's them," I said. I already knew what Mom's next question would be.

"How do you know them?" she asked, surprise evident in her voice.

Look at that. I was right.

I had a slight inward panic at that question, hoping she wouldn't be able to put two and two together and figure out that I was the one who had danced with them. I calmly explained, "I ran into them the first day we were here, and we've run into each other some other times. I've hung out with them a little. They seem pretty cool."

"Oh, okay," she said. I waited for my mom to say something else, but to my surprise she remained quiet. *I guess that's the end of that.*

We got into the rental car, and Mom asked, "How about we drive around until we find a place where we want to eat, then we can go find a dress and mask. Sound good?"

I smiled at my mom and said, "Sounds great." Mom pulled out of the hotel and started driving. After a short while into the drive, I spotted a small diner that looked good. "What about there?" I asked, pointing out the diner.

"That looks good," Mom responded. She pulled into the parking lot.

We perused the menu in a comfortable silence. The waitress came and got our drink and food order, since we already knew what we wanted.

When the waitress departed from the table, Mom was the first one to speak. "How have you enjoyed the trip so far?" My knee-jerk reaction would be to say that it had been unenjoyable, since we hadn't had a lot of family time. But I had a different response.

"In all honesty, I've enjoyed it a lot more than I thought I would. How about you?" I asked her.

"It's been a lot of work, but it's been enjoyable. I'm looking forward to some time with the family though." I nodded in agreement. "You've spent a decent amount of time with those boys I saw in the lobby?" she inquired with a knowing smile.

I nodded again. "Yeah, they're really nice. I haven't spent all my time with them, but it's been nice not to be by myself while you guys are all too busy." Before I could catch myself, I realized what had just slipped out. I instantly regretted my words. I became increasingly interested in my napkin, trying to avoid Mom's gaze. I didn't know what would upset her more: me hanging out with a group of guys without her permission, or me taking a stab at her. The truth was, I didn't really blame them for being too busy.

My mom sensed my concern. "Kinsley, sweetie, I'm not upset with you. I expected you to make a friend or two while we were here, and I want you to know that we haven't been trying to leave you out this week. We've all been wishing we could spend more time with you. We all just have had a lot to do," she said in a soft tone.

I met my mom's gaze and smiled. For some reason, I felt the need to share with my mom what had been going through my head since we'd arrived. However, it was not exactly easy to share about my insecurities. I wasn't sure how my mom would take my feelings.

"I know. It's just…hard sometimes being the only one who isn't in the arts industry." I could tell I had all of Mom's attention, as she hung onto my every word. "Sometimes it makes me feel left out…or inadequate."

I searched my mom's face, waiting for her response. I wondered if I had made the wrong decision to discuss this with her, but somehow I also knew telling her was the right thing.

"I get that. We never want you to feel left out. You are as much a part of this family as anyone else, and you are not inadequate. Being in the industry doesn't make you special; just being you makes you special. You are so bright and talented. You're more creative than I could ever be, and you're as good or possibly an even better dancer than that YouTuber." I let out a short laugh at that last part. *You have no idea.*

"How would you know if I'm any good? You've never seen me dance," I said with amusement. I knew what my mom was going to say next. "The one class I took when I was six doesn't count."

Mom gave me her signature mom look. I knew then and there I wasn't going to be able to argue with what came next.

"It does count. You had a natural talent then; you have natural talent now. You were the best in that class. So maybe I don't know if you are currently as good as that dancer. What I do know is if you had lessons, you could be better than that dancer." I scanned my mom's face for any sign of a lie. Her eyes were sincere. She truly believed I was that good.

"Well, I'm not sure I'd go that far," *considering I couldn't be better than her because I am her,* "but thanks, Mom."

My mind wanted to say instantly, *she's your mom; she has to say that.* But then it dawned on me: she didn't have to say that. No rule in life says your mom has to give you false praise. In fact, I knew a lot of kids whose parents never complimented them for any skills. Plus, I had heard I was a good dancer from Advanced Company; well Incognito heard it, but it was the same thing.

Mom was right. Just being in the arts industry didn't make anyone special. Many talented people were not in that industry.

I was pulled from my thoughts when the waitress came and dropped off Mom's big chicken dish and my giant salad.

Apparently, this place is generous with their portions. We thanked the waitress and dug into our meals..

"Now the important question: have you developed a crush on any of these guys?" she asked.

I laughed. My mom was forever interested in girl talk—and always wanting to know if I liked someone. She had nothing to worry about; I wasn't looking to date, let alone like anyone anytime soon. It took too much time and effort to date someone.

"No, Mom. We're just friends. That's it, and that's all it will be. Besides I don't even know exactly where they live. I know they live in California, but I forgot to ask where, and California's a huge state. Chances are I'll never see them again. Plus, I barely know them."

To which my mom responded, "Hey, I've heard of a lot of long-distance relationships that have worked." I rolled my eyes and laughed, knowing that was a joke.

"What color dress were you thinking?" my mom asked, changing the subject.

"To be honest, I hadn't thought about it," I shrugged.

Mom wasn't surprised one bit by my answer. "Alright, we'll just see what we can find."

Chapter 21

We got in the car, and Mom asked, "Since we don't know this area at all, I figured we could do the same thing we did to find breakfast: drive around exploring the area until we find a shop we want to go in. Sound good?"

"Sounds good to me," I reassured. Mom nodded and pulled out of the diner's parking lot. Most normal people would just use their smartphone to look up a place to shop or eat, but my family commonly used this method instead. We had more of an adventure that way.

We drove farther into town, and everything was just a blur to me. I wasn't thinking about getting a dress. My thoughts drifted back to what my mom had said: "You're an even better dancer than that YouTuber." I realized my mom and dad wanted me to be in the industry, because they thought I was talented. They wanted me to recognize my talent. They weren't trying to put me in the industry so I would be popular or just like the rest of the family.

I do enjoy dancing an awful lot. I guess I could consider the idea of taking some dance classes and working toward becoming a professional dancer. I mean, Incognito is popular, and I don't believe it's just because of her mask, so maybe I have the potential to be a dancer.

I was pulled from my thoughts as I heard my mom begin to speak. "What about here?" She pointed out a small little dress shop.

"Sure," was all I said. I wasn't an experienced dress shopper. A dress was a dress to me. I mean, I'd worn plenty of dresses before, but I didn't know what qualified as a good place to get a dress—especially for something of this scale. That was my mom's department.

"We have plenty of time, so you can try on whatever you want to, and we can even go to another store if we need to," Mom said as we were walking in.

Oh please no, I don't want to have to go to a whole bunch of stores and lose my entire day. I replied with a simple, "Okay."

We entered the shop, and I was surprised by all the different dresses. I thought to myself that they had any color you could imagine and every style that ever existed.

"What color do you lean toward?" Mom asked me.

"Um...I guess black, red, green, or blue." She acknowledged my response and instantly started looking for dresses for me.

I started absentmindedly glancing through dresses. I looked through dress after dress, occasionally finding cute ones, but nothing I was crazy about or would want to wear. After a while searching through racks and pulling one or two out occasionally, I went over to my mom to find she had grabbed a few as well.

"You ready to go try these on?" she asked.

"Yeah, if I get any more, my arms may break under the weight," I said.

We made our way back to the dressing rooms. I looked at the dresses and smiled. *My mom knows me better than to pull out a traditional ball gown-styled dress.* None of the dresses were the puffy style, which I mentally thanked her for as I slipped on the first one. It was a sparkly, light-blue, floor-length dress. I thought I was going to like it because of the color, but it wasn't flattering on me.

I stepped out of the dressing room to show my mom. She shook her head. I kept trying on dress after dress. Anything from green to pink, mermaid style to high-lows. I came to the last dress—with my hopes low, since all the other dresses didn't look right.

Maybe I am the problem, not the dresses. Maybe nothing will look good on me.

The last dress was a deep red that appeared rather plain on the hanger. The dress had a halter neckline and an open back. The straps crossed in the back. Rhinestones adorned around the neckline and along the waistline.

I slipped the dress on and smiled at my reflection. It was perfect. I stepped out to show my mom, and when I came out, she smiled immediately.

"That's the one!" she said bursting with enthusiasm. I nodded in agreement.

I changed back into my clothes, glad to finally be done. We bought the dress and left. Once in the car, my mom brought up the hard part, "Now for the difficult part: we have to find you a mask."

"Yeah, I have no clue where to go," I said exasperatedly.

My mom thought for a minute and suggested, "Why don't we look up the closest mall and go see if any of their accessory stores have one? It's a long shot, but it's worth a try, right?"

"Yeah, sounds like a plan," I said.

We looked up the closest mall, and Mom started to drive there. I guess I hadn't considered that I couldn't wear my mask. *Not only does it not match the dress, but my family would know I was Incognito.*

We arrived at the mall and started to wander around, looking for a store that sold masks. We went to one store and asked if they had any masquerade masks. To our disappointment, they didn't. However, the person working did recommend another store we could try.

We worked our way across the mall. As we approached the recommended shop, I saw it was an accessory store with everything from hats, belts, scarfs, jewelry, and everything in-between.

Mom asked the salesperson, "Do you guys happen to carry masquerade masks?"

"We do. They are over on the back wall over there." the lady pointed to the masks. Mom thanked her, and we made our way to the back wall. The selection was small, but at least they had some.

I wasn't sure which one I wanted. As I looked over the masks, eventually one jumped out to me. This mask was entirely different than the one I usually wore. It was black and only covered my eyes and a little bit of my right cheek. The top was scalloped, and the sides were slightly pointed. The mask had red lace over it—and red and black rhinestones on it.

I picked up the mask and showed it to my mom. "What about this one?"

"That one's great. It looks like it would match your dress perfectly!" I smiled at her response. We checked out and headed back to the car.

It suddenly occurred to me we didn't get my mom a dress or mask. "What about you?" I asked.

"What about me?" she asked, slightly confused.

"We didn't get you a dress or mask."

"I brought one of my dresses from home. I knew there was going to be a masquerade at the end. I didn't tell you, because I thought it would be fun to have a nice day out shopping—just you and me. Plus, I thought you deserved a new dress," she explained.

I smiled. "Thank you. I'm glad I got to have a girls day with you."

"Me too, it was quite enjoyable," she said.

We parked the car and headed up to our room. As we stood to wait for the elevator, my mom broke the silence. "You know, since you're going to the masquerade, that means I get to do your hair and makeup."

I groaned. "No one's even going to see my face. Can't we skip the makeup? It would be pointless anyway." I tried my best to persuade her.

"You still see the majority of your face, and masks don't hide your eyes. People will still be able to see your eyes." Mom countered my argument.

The elevator arrived, we stepped on, and Mom pressed our floor number while trying to encourage me. "It's not that bad, you know."

"Maybe to you; you're used to wearing makeup. You know I don't like having to wear it; it itches."

"It's just this once. I think you'll live." Mom looked at me with her signature mom look.

"I don't have a choice, do I? " I said, defeated.

"No. No, you don't," Mom said as the elevator doors opened.

Chapter 22

With time to kill before the masquerade, I decided to hang out in my room for a little bit. I logged on Incognito's Twitter and saw a few people had tweeted about her—or, well, me. The tweets were all about the performance with Advanced Company. I began to read them.

"Incognito killed it with Advanced Company."

"I couldn't tell who was the newbie and who was the pro."

It gave me a sense of pride that people liked the performance. I tweeted back the people who had tweeted me.

Then I saw that I—or should I say Incognito—had a private message. I opened my messages and saw it was from Justin. The message read, "Hey, great job yesterday."

I instantly replied, "Thanks, you guys were amazing!"

"Thanks, you would have never known it was your first time performing," Justin responded.

His message made me smile. "Thanks for the encouragement."

After I sent that message, I logged off and entered the family room to find everyone but Darren.

"Where's Darren?" I asked.

"He went to roam the hotel, most likely to fail at picking up chicks," Ty said, not looking up from his phone. I couldn't help but laugh at Ty's explanation of Darren's disappearance. My parents laughed as well.

"Are you ready to start preparing for the masquerade?" Mom asked.

"As ready as I can be to be shoved into a dress and have paint caked on my face," I deadpanned.

Dad laughed, and Mom shot a glare Dad's way before saying, "You're so dramatic. Come on, let's get started."

She grabbed my hand and started to pull me off toward her room. As she did, I turned to Dad, and Ty and mouthed, "*Help me,*" to which I heard them laugh as the door to Mom's room shut.

Mom started with my hair. She did a simple yet elegant up-do. She worked a crown braid back into a soft bun. It didn't take her very long to finish with my hair and start on my makeup.

As she was about to start, I stopped her. "Not that much, okay?"

She chuckled. "I know, don't worry; I'm just gonna do a little," she reassured me.

Putting on my makeup took a little longer than doing my hair. I waited patiently though, not saying a word. My mom finally put on the finishing touches.

"Okay, you're all done. Go get your dress on," she commanded. I obeyed and got up to put on my dress. When I entered the bathroom, I kept my eyes away from the mirror. Not that that it was a hard thing to do; I usually avoided looking in mirrors. *I don't usually like what I find staring back at me. All I can ever see are my flaws.*

When I emerged from the bathroom in my dress to show my mom, her face opened into a wide smile. "You look stunning!" she gushed.

"Thanks," I said. I braved the mirror for the first time and was amazed at what I found. I almost didn't look like myself. "Man, Mom. You're a miracle worker." I couldn't believe how I looked. *For once, my flaws weren't the first thing I noticed. I was struck by my vibrant green eyes.* Mom had masterfully drawn attention to my eyes with her dramatic use of eyeliner and eyeshadow.

"No, you're just naturally beautiful. What little makeup I put on only complements that," Mom said lovingly. I smiled and hugged her, not having any words. "Now for the finishing touch," she said as she crossed over to the dresser and grabbed my new mask.

She skillfully helped me put it on. Once my mask was on, I looked in the mirror again. The mask matched the dress perfectly. For once in my life, I was happy I'd let my mother take me shopping and do my makeup. I felt like the princess my dad thought I was, and Mom was who made that happen.

I guess it's true that what people want isn't always what's best for them. I wanted to skip shopping and the masquerade all together, but then I would have missed a bonding experience with my mom and missed this moment of actually feeling pretty.

In the midst of getting me ready, Mom had somehow found time to get ready herself. She hadn't put her mask on yet, but she was in her dress with her hair and makeup done.

"Now let's go show your father," Mom said.

I walked out to the family room to find Dad, Darren, and Ty—all dressed up. Dad went with the classic black and white tuxedo, and he had a white mask in his hand.

Darren had gone with a more dramatic look with an all-blacked-out look: black mask with a black on black tux. Even his shirt and bow tie were black.

Ty went with a more fun look given his age. He dawned a sapphire blue tuxedo with a matching mask in his hand. I wasn't surprised at all with how well Ty could pull it off. His attire matched his youthful energy. They all looked up from what they were doing and had different expressions of surprise or shock.

Dad was the first to speak up. "You look amazing, Kins. Like a real princess," he said, smiling at me.

I returned the smile. "Thanks, Dad."

Both of my brothers were in shock. Darren managed to say something before Ty did. "Who even knew you could clean up?" Darren said, teasing me.

"Oh shut up. I'm surprised you even know what dress clothes are," I said, firing back.

Darren laughed. "In all seriousness, you look good," he said honestly.

"Same with you," I said.

Ty finally spoke up. "You look pretty, sis.'"

I smiled and hugged Ty. "Thanks, and you look very handsome," I said, complimenting my brother. Ty smiled and thanked me in return.

"Well, it seems we're all ready. Shall we go?" Dad asked.

We all responded with either head nods or yeses. We trooped off toward the conference wing. As we walked to where the masquerade was held, I saw other people in masks on their way. *At least I know we're not late.*

I felt so nervous I was almost sick to my stomach. This was much worse than performing. Having to mingle in a room full of performers, managers, agents, and even some casting directors was terrifying. I was about to be in a sea of faceless strangers.

I don't like crowds on a regular basis, let alone when you can't tell who anyone is.

We reached the door to the room of the masquerade, and before entering, I took a deep breath.

Here goes nothing.

Chapter 23

The moment I stepped foot into the room, my mouth dropped in awe. It was a huge ballroom I hadn't been in yet. A band played on a small stage. Black chandeliers with crystals hung from the ceiling. The dark floor was offset by light designs, with a large dance floor made from dark wood in the center of the room.

Thick red curtains framed both sides of the stage, and a black curtain hung along the backside, much like at a theater. Tables lined the perimeter of the dance floor. No one was dancing at that moment.

Every color and style of dress imaginable and masks of every kind graced the room. I was overwhelmed by all of it. My thoughts wandered: *I am at an actual masquerade ball.* Everyone was dressed up; most of the girls had full-on ball gowns. Thankfully, I wasn't the only one who went with a more understated look, so I didn't look totally out of place.

"What do you think?" Mom asked my brothers and me.

Since I was kind of speechless at that moment, Ty answered first. "It's awesome!"

Darren went with a more subtle response: "It's cool." In Darren-speak, that was equivalent to Ty's *awesome.*

My mom looked at me. "What about you, Kinsley?"

"Oh, it's incredible," I marveled at the room. I was still caught up in looking around, and I didn't notice my brothers depart. I just looked up, and they were gone. I assumed they had gone off to find whatever friends they had made during the week.

I glanced at my parents to find them already talking to two important looking people; they had already removed their masks and were sitting at a table, intently discussing something.

Here I am, left by myself again.

I was tempted just to leave then and there, but I decided against it. I might as well try and have fun. I perused the dance floor and saw quite a few people had started dancing. Everyone was slow dancing with a partner at that moment. *Well, no way am I joining in on that—because let's be real, I'm not going to ask someone to dance, and there's no way anyone is going to ask me.*

I started walking around the room, and my mind wandered to Advanced Company. *Could they be here? They weren't contestants in the showcase though, and they didn't even know this was happening. Besides, why would they come to a ball where they didn't know anyone and didn't have much to do with the showcase? Is it strange that I wish they were here?*

I was brought out of my thoughts when I spotted Rachel, who wasn't wearing a mask, and went up to compliment her on what a wonderful job she'd done with the event. I saw she was talking to a man and wondered if I should wait for them to finish talking, but I didn't know how long she would be and I knew I would be quick. *Plus, don't you expect to have people join and leave your conversation often at these things?* I told myself.

I mustered up courage, walked over to Rachel, and said, "Excuse me," hoping to get her attention.

"Hi, can I help you?" she asked.

I don't think she recognizes who I am, but then again isn't that kind of the point of a masquerade?

"I just wanted to tell you what an amazing job you did tonight."

"Oh, thank you so much. You know..." Just then, Rachel was cut off by someone else coming up to talk to her.

I looked to my left and saw the guy she had been talking to was also still there.

"I'm sorry for interrupting. It seems now you can't finish your conversation with her," I said apologetically.

The mystery man just smiled. "No worries. We weren't talking about anything serious. Now if you'll excuse me, I have someone I must go find."

"Good luck finding whoever it is in this sea of masks," I said as he walked off.

Again, I was alone in a room full of faceless strangers. I continued to walk the perimeter of the dance floor, and I wished I had enough courage to ask someone to dance with me. I heard the band stop playing and saw Rachel walk up on stage.

"Hello everyone, I'm glad you could make it. This is both a thank you of sorts for everything you've done this weekend, and a chance for everyone to mingle without feeling intimidated by who they're talking to." A wave of soft chuckles rolled across the room.

Rachel continued to talk, and I tuned her out eventually—not purposely, it just kind of happened as my mind began to wander.

As I zoned out, I felt someone step next to me. I looked to my left and saw a guy wearing a tux with a slate grey jacket and black pants who seemed about my age, though it was hard to tell through his mask since it covered most his face.

The image of him snapped me out of my daze. I went back to listening to Rachel.

"Now, since we are in a room full of performers and many talented dancers, I wanted to invite those to the dance floor who know how to waltz."

Rachel exited the stage, and the band started to play. Couples made their way to the dance floor and began to waltz—some better than others. I stood in awe, wishing I knew how to waltz.

"Pretty amazing, huh?" the guy beside me asked.

"It's incredible," I said in awe, not taking my eyes off the dancers.

"Would you like to join me?" the guy said as he held out his hand for me to take it.

My head snapped in his direction. "What? Me? No, I couldn't. I don't know how to waltz," I said stumbling over my words. *Real smooth, Kinsley.*

The guy smiled. "All you need is a good partner who knows what he's doing. Lucky for you, I just happen to know how to waltz," he persuaded.

Chapter 24

My gaze followed the mystery guy's extended hand back up to his grinning face. I wanted to dance, but I didn't want to make a fool of myself.

The mystery guy picked up on my uneasiness. "You have nothing to worry about. I have a feeling you'll do better than half the people who are already dancing. We'll start simple," he said, reassuring me.

I decided to get out of my head and just act like I was more confident than I felt. I reached out and took his hand. His grin grew into a full-on smile. He led me to the dance floor, and we got into the waltz hold. That was about the only part of the waltz I knew how to do. "Just let me lead," he instructed before we started.

I nodded my head, showing I understood, and we began to waltz. He kept talking me through every step. I fumbled over my feet the first few steps. I think the stumbling was due more to how awkward I felt dancing with a stranger than my actual dancing ability.

Once I ignored the awkwardness, I got the hang of the simple steps, so he tried changing it up a little. I followed quite well. It was a lot of fun; everyone else on the floor faded away, and it was just him and me focused on dancing. Dancing with a partner made my mind flash back to dancing with Justin. *This feels strangely similar.*

As we danced, I couldn't help but feel like I knew this masked mystery man somehow. I studied his face, trying to recognize anything that would tip me off to who he was. He had light blue eyes with flecks of green in them. I remember seeing these exact eyes before, but I just couldn't place them. His mask was throwing me off.

"Enjoying the view?" he joked when he caught me studying his face. I could feel my cheeks heat up. I darted my gaze down to the floor and then back up to his face.

I quickly thought of a way to change the conversation topic and focus it away from me. "How is it you know how to waltz so well? Are you a dancer?"

"It just so happens that I am. What about you? You've picked up the dance faster than most. Are you a dancer?"

"No, I'm not in a dance studio or pursuing a career in dance. I just enjoy dancing—though I don't typically dance in public or waltz with masked strangers," I said, letting a slight smile grace my lips.

"Oh, so your stage is your bedroom, and you usually only dance with unmasked strangers," he said with a light tone.

I laughed at his joke.

Before I could respond, he continued, "Why?"

"Why what?" I asked, confused by his question.

"Why not be in a dance studio or pursue a career in dance if you love it so much?" I could see the curiosity shining in his eyes.

"It's complicated," was all I said. Before he could ask me anything else about it, I changed the conversation topic. "Anyhow, I don't believe I got your name?"

He gave me a slight smirk. "Where's the fun in that? Honestly, I'm surprised you don't know." I looked at him in confusion. He continued, "I figured you were more perceptive than that."

He was about to say something else, and the song changed. I looked around and saw there were fewer couples on the dance floor—most of them starting an almost contemporary-like dance. You could tell the only people remaining on the floor were actual dancers.

I started to walk away, only for the mystery guy to grab my hand and turn me back around. "Who said you had to quit dancing just because the song changed?"

"I'm not a dancer. These people are all clearly dancers," I said, gesturing toward the dancers.

"I bet you could give them a run for their money. I have a feeling you know how to dance to this," he said with confidence. When I didn't speak, he said, "Just move to the rhythm, and I'll join in. Just ignore the others."

I studied him closely for a minute as he let go of my hand. *What could it hurt to try dancing? It's not like anyone can see my face, and no one will know it is me if I make a fool out of myself.* I took a step back and started to dance to the music. The mystery guy soon fell perfectly in sync. We danced through the entire song. When the song switched to something entirely different, we just switched our style of dance.

After about three songs, we decided to take a break. As we exited the dance floor, I noticed quite a few people had been watching us specifically. I guess we drew some attention.

Once we were off the dance floor, I was the first one to speak. "Thank you, that was a lot of fun. You were incredible," I said, complimenting him.

"Thanks, so were you. No one would ever know you weren't a dancer," he complimented me back.

It occurred to me he never told me who he was, yet he seemed to somehow know who I was. "Who are you? You seem like you already know me pretty well." I hadn't met anyone in the showcase, and Advanced Company couldn't be there.

"Why don't I just show you?" he said as he reached up to remove his mask.

Chapter 25

The mystery man removed his mask, and before me stood the person I had been getting to know over the past several days: Justin's face came into view. I got lost in thought for a moment. *I guess Advanced Company was here. It makes sense why he could dance so well, and why we danced so well together. It also explains why dancing with him reminded me of Incognito dancing with Justin.*

I knew his eyes and voice were familiar. However, I had told myself it couldn't be him because he wasn't supposed to be there.

"What are you doing here? Are the others here as well?" I asked, still in shock.

"Well, remember how we performed for the dance portion?" I just nodded my head, hoping he would continue. "We ran into Rachel yesterday, and she invited us. We all thought it could be fun, and we figured you would be here, so we all came."

I was about to respond, but then it occurred to me: dancing with me, he could be assuming I was Incognito Moves, or he could be thinking I was Kinsley. *I need to figure out who he thinks I am before I say something that makes him figure out that I'm both of them.* Sheer panic coursed through my body. *What if he finds out? What if he tells the others? What if while dancing with me, he figured it out? Okay, calm down Kinsley. Just ask him who he thinks you are.*

"I'm not sure I'm convinced that you know who I am. Who is it you believe you're talking to?" I inquired.

"Really Kinsley, I'm hurt that you have such little faith in me," he said, placing a hand over his heart as if I had wounded him.

I mentally released a sigh of relief. "I'm impressed that you could find me in this crowd and figure out who I was," I said.

Even though Justin knew who I was, I still didn't feel like taking my mask off. Something about my mask just felt safe.

"Well, I'm impressed with how well you dance, for someone who has never been trained. You're almost as good as some pros," Justin complimented. I smiled but also remembered hearing similar comments about Incognito.

I'm still a little worried that he's put two and two together.

"Thanks, I guess it just comes naturally." I hesitated before continuing and asking my next question. "What made you want to ask me to dance? How did you know that I would be able to keep up?" I was worried about what his response would be.

"I came over and stood by you, because from behind I thought it was you. Once I was standing beside you, I figured out you were indeed who I thought you were. I could tell how badly you wanted to be out there dancing. Plus, I've always had a hunch that you were at least a pretty decent dancer, given that you love dance, and you have a talented family."

I nodded, taking in what he had said. "I'm honestly surprised that you didn't figure out it was me," Justin said.

"Well, in my defense, I didn't think you guys would be here."

"Yeah, that's fair. I'll give you that one," Justin said.

"I wondered if it was you for a little bit, but I reminded myself that you guys wouldn't be here," I said, explaining why I seemed oblivious.

Before Justin could respond, three guys in masks, who I assumed was the rest of Advanced Company, walked up to us. The shortest one, in a tux with a dark green jacket and black pants, spoke first.

"Who's this?" Between his height and voice, I knew it was Tommy.

Justin and I looked at each other with a knowing smile.

The other two studied Justin and me, trying to figure out who I was, when the one in a classic black pinstriped tux said, "You look great, Kinsley." Since he was the only blonde, I knew it was Adam.

I felt my cheeks get slightly hot. I wasn't used to getting compliments about how I looked; it made me somewhat uncomfortable.

"Thank you, Adam. You're too kind." Tommy and the one in a dark blue tux—which I realized was Nick—just stood there in slight confusion, still not putting two and two together. I finally got the courage to remove my mask and place it on the table next to us to help them put the pieces together.

"Oooh, that makes sense. We all wondered how Justin dared to ask a girl to dance!" Nick said, elbowing Justin.

I slightly chuckled and looked at Justin, who was rubbing the back of his neck. "How did Justin and Adam figure out who you are, and I didn't?" Nick complained.

"We pay attention, unlike some people," Adam said, poking fun at Nick.

"I pay attention!" Nick said in defense.

"Yeah—to *yourself*," Justin said, joining the teasing.

I smiled as I watched them squabble back and forth. Suddenly, I could tell Adam liked the song that had just came on. I noticed him look at me and then hesitantly extend his hand. "Care to dance?"

I smiled and took his hand. "I would love to."

Adam guided me to the dance floor before I could grab my mask, so I realized the whole room would be able to tell who I was; but I reminded myself no one in the room knew me anyway, other than my family and Advanced Company. I was able to calm my thoughts and have a good time.

After a little while, Nick sauntered up. "Mind if I cut in?" he asked.

"Not at all," Adam said. He thanked me for the dance and stepped away. Nick goofed off for the majority of the dance, and I laughed at his antics.

Tommy came over as the song was changing, "May I have this dance?" he asked, all gentleman-like.

"Of course you may," I responded.

I had such a good time dancing with Tommy. He was sweet and funny. The song switched again, and I had planned to keep dancing, but Tommy stopped. "Thanks for dancing with me, Kinsley. I enjoyed it, but now it's someone else turn," Tommy said before walking away.

I wasn't sure what he meant by someone else's turn; no one had asked to cut in, so I was left on the dance floor alone. Just then, I felt someone take my hand and spin me around. I came face to face with Justin. I blushed, noticing how close we had gotten when he spun me.

"Shall we?" Justin asked. I nodded in response—too flustered to form a coherent sentence.

It was strange not having my mask on while dancing with Justin. I felt exposed, yet comfortable at the same time. I didn't have to hide who I was. Dancing with him was almost effortless. Our steps matched perfectly. When I danced with the other guys, they goofed off and joked. Justin was different.

We talked throughout the entire dance. Justin didn't joke as the others did, but he kept things light and playful. At the same time, the conversation was more than just small talk. In the middle of our conversation, Justin stopped talking and studied my face. His intense gaze started to make me feel uncomfortable; I had to break eye contact by glancing away.

After I looked away, Justin spoke. "Your eyes are stunning." I was floored at Justin's bold compliment.

"I…um… thank you," I stammered, keeping my eyes glued to the floor. *He likes my eyes. Not my dress or my mask. My eyes.* It felt good to know he liked the one thing on me that was a part of me. He singled out the one thing that hadn't changed from a normal basis—my eyes.

The song ended, and we walked off the dance floor, back to where our masks were. We all decided to put our masks back on, since we were at a masquerade, after all.

"You guys have made tonight a lot of fun, but I really should go find my family since its getting late," I said reluctantly.

"Thank you for dancing with us. We'll see you around," Justin said with a smile. They all said their various "byes" and "see you arounds."

I walked away and started searching for my family. I had made it to the other side of the room, where I found Dad talking to someone. I patiently waited for him to finish, since it sounded important.

Dad finished the conversation, and I spoke up. "Hey Dad, where's everyone else?"

"Your brothers just went back to the room, and your mother—" he turned around to point toward her, and she was gone, "I'm not sure where she went. We were waiting for you to be ready to leave before we went back to the room, but it appears I've lost your mother."

I smiled. "You seem to lose mom a lot," I joked.

A slow song came on, and I looked at Dad and smiled. He instantly knew what I was thinking.

"Kinsley, I'm not a dancer," he said, warning me.

"That doesn't matter," I replied.

"All right then, if you don't care about being embarrassed—would you care to dance?" He offered me his hand.

I responded with a big smile as I accepted his hand. "I would love to."

He escorted me to the dance floor. As we danced, I couldn't help but think back to when I was younger, and I would always ask him to dance with me. It didn't matter what he was doing, he would stop just to dance with me. He would guide me around the room as I fumbled on my feet.

I miss the simpler times as a child when my world was carefree, and I didn't have to impress anyone.

We talked most of the time, just enjoying ourselves. Once the song finished, we walked off the dance floor.

"What do you mean, you're *not a dancer*? You were great!" I said.

He smiled. "Well, you had to get your dancing talent from somewhere," he said, just as Mom walked up.

"Yes, and that somewhere is me," she stated, smiling.

"Yeah, Dad, you're good, but she has you beat," I said. We all laughed.

"Ready to go back to the room?" Dad asked. I nodded my head, and my mom said yes.

When we got to the room, Ty and Darren were in the family room already, changed out of dress clothes and watching TV. I told my family I was going to change and go to bed, because I was exhausted.

Once in my room, I took off my mask and let my hair down. I then changed into my soft pajamas and washed the makeup off my face. I lay in bed, and my mind buzzed with excitement. *The rest of the week I get to enjoy family time.* Despite my excited state, I could tell it wouldn't be long before sleep would overtake me.

Chapter 26

I woke up, instantly remembering that this day would mark the start of our family time.

I don't have a clue what my parents have planned for today, but that doesn't matter. I'm just excited to get their dedicated time.

I jumped out of bed, got ready for the day, and dashed to the family room to find everyone there but Ty.

"Good morning, princess," Dad said.

"Good morning," I responded. I took the only empty seat in the family room. "Let me guess. Ty is still asleep?" I asked, already knowing the answer.

"You guessed correctly," Mom said with a smile.

Darren took out his headphones and asked, "When are we going to get breakfast? I'm starving."

"Oh yes, you're withering away to nothing," I replied with a smirk. Darren shot me a glare.

"Well, we can wake Ty up and go now," Dad said.

"Then what are we waiting for?" Darren asked as he stood up.

"We're waiting for you to wake up Ty," Dad said.

Darren paused, "What?"

"We'll leave now, but you have to wake up Ty. That's the deal," Dad stated, as though he were negotiating a business deal.

Darren sighed. "Fine."

Darren disappeared into his room. I smiled, knowing all too well how upset Ty would be with Darren for waking him up. No one wanted that job.

"Nice one," I said to Dad. He winked back at me.

After a short while, Darren came out of the room. "How did it go?" I questioned.

"Oh you know, he thinks I'm the worst human being on the planet and has officially shunned me for all eternity." I laughed, knowing all too well that was probably not an exaggeration of what had come out of Ty's mouth.

Moments later, Ty trudged out of his room, scowling and not saying a word.

"Alright, seems like everyone is ready; let's go," Mom said, standing up.

"Some are ready more willingly than others," Darren whispered to me. I stifled my laugh. Dad just grinned at us but didn't say anything.

As we made our way to the elevator, I wondered if I would see Advanced Company at breakfast. We rode the elevator to the lobby and entered the dining area. I looked around and didn't see any sign of Advanced Company. I wasn't sure if I was glad I didn't see them so my family time wouldn't be interrupted, or if I was a little bummed.

I quickly shook the thought out of my head and got my food. I set my plate of eggs and bacon down on the table and went to fetch my glass of orange juice. I was the first to sit down at the table. Mom sat down next with her oatmeal and fruit. The boys sat down at the same time.

Darren and Dad had piled their plates with basically the same stuff: sausage, bacon, eggs, and a waffle. The only difference in meals was that Dad was drinking coffee and Darren was drinking orange juice.

Ty was an entirely different story; his plate consisted of a small pile of pancakes and bacon, with his cup full of apple juice.

Everyone was quiet as they ate, until Darren asked, "What are our plans for today?"

"We don't have any. We wanted to let you guys decide," Mom said.

Before Darren could even get a response in, Ty cut in: "I want to go to the water park!" His eyes shone with enthusiasm.

"That could be fun," Darren agreed.

"What do you think, Kinsley?" Dad asked.

The water park wouldn't have been my first pick, but who was I to kill my little brother's hopes and dreams?

"Sure," was all I said.

"It's settled then; we'll go to the water park," Dad announced. We finished our breakfast and headed back upstairs to change. We quickly put on our swimsuits and made the trek to the water park.

We entered the water park and scoped out a set of chairs. We quickly were able to find enough chairs for all of us. Once everyone had gotten their stuff situated, it was time to decide what to do first.

"Where to?" I asked. Everyone took a minute to look around at the slides.

I was surprised when Dad spoke up first. "What about that slide?" he pointed at a red body slide.

"I'm down," Darren said.

"Sure," Ty and I said at the same time.

We marched off toward the slide and entered the line. It moved quickly. Once we were close to the top, I saw that there were two different slides.

"Why don't we race?" Darren said, announcing what I was thinking.

"Sure," I said.

"I want to race too!" Ty jumped in.

"I think you kids need to step aside for the master racer," Dad said with confidence.

"Oh, really? I think you may have just met your match," Darren replied with fire in his voice.

"Then what are you waiting for?" Dad asked while motioning to the slides.

Darren and Dad disappeared first down the slide.

"Will you race me?" Ty pleaded with puppy dog eyes.

"I would love to race you, but do you think you can handle it?" I said, challenging Ty.

"Oh yeah. I think you're the one who won't be able to handle losing," Ty fired back. I looked at Mom and saw she was smiling at our banter.

The lifeguard waved us forward, and Ty and I went to our separate slides. The lifeguard gave us the all-clear, and I waited just a second before starting down the slide. I was hoping to provide Ty with some extra time.

He enjoys winning more than I do, and I enjoy seeing him happy. Its a win-win situation, I thought.

I ejected from my slide, and judging by where Ty was and how happy he seemed, I realized he had beat me by just a few seconds.

"I won!" Ty said, pumping his fist in the air.

"It appears you did!" I said when I reached the boys. "Who won out of you two?" I asked; however, just by looking at the irritation on Darren's face, I already knew the answer.

"Good question; who did win, Darren?" Dad asked Darren with a smirk.

Darren looked less than amused. "You just got lucky," Darren grumbled.

"Oh, is that what you're calling it? Because I would call it *skill*," Dad said, pushing Darren's buttons. I smiled at Dad's joking ways.

Mom joined the group and proceeded to ask, "Who won?"

Ty was quick to answer for our race, "I did," pointing at himself.

"What about you two?" Mom asked the two older guys.

Dad smirked and pointed his thumbs at himself. "This guy," he said. Darren rolled his eyes, and I let out a chuckle.

"Ty, you won our race; do you want to pick where we go next?" I asked.

"Yes!" He bounced up and down with excitement.

He looked around the water park until he found a slide that he thought seemed fun. He chose the slide with the big inner tube that seated six people. I remembered that ride from when just Ty and Darren had come with me.

Once we reached the top, Dad asked Ty, "Are you ready for this?" with the excitement of a young child.

"Oh yeah. I was born ready," Ty matched Dad's enthusiasm.

The lifeguard waved us forward, and we all situated our bodies in the inner tube. The lifeguard gave the inner tube a light push forward, and down the slide we went. Just like the last time, Darren and Ty whooped and hollered throughout, only this time Dad joined in.

Mom and I laughed almost the entire way down at the boy's shenanigans. Once out of the slide, Ty started rambling about how fun it was and how with more people, it was even better than last time.

Mom declared that she was going to the lazy river, and we all decided to join for a bit. After some time in the river, Ty, of course, got bored and asked Darren and me to do more slides with him.

"We'll meet you guys back at our stuff?" I asked.

"Sounds good," Mom said.

The boys and I headed off to tackle more slides. Any slide we could, we raced. I, of course, lost every time to Darren and let Ty beat me a few times. After quite a few slides, I figured it best to head back to our stuff and see if Mom and Dad were there yet.

Darren and Ty agreed. As we got closer to our chairs, I could see that Mom and Dad were already there. Mom was reading a book, and Dad was on his phone.

I got my love of reading from my mom, possibly one of the only things we have in common.

We reached our spot, and I sat down in my chair.

"Did you guys have fun?" Dad asked.

I didn't even bother trying to respond. I knew Ty would beat me to it. "It was awesome!" he cheered. Ty then continued to rave about how fun it was and describe all the slides we'd gone on. He proudly shared how many times he'd won.

After we had sat and chatted for a while, Dad looked at the time. "It's 3:30. Do you guys want to change and then head into town for dinner and some time to explore?" he suggested.

"Sounds great," Mom said.

"I'm in," Ty stated.

"Eh, why not?" was Darren's non-enthusiastic response.

"What are we waiting for?" I said as I got up and gathered my stuff. *I wonder what our excursion into the city will hold?*

Chapter 27

The hotel wasn't far from downtown. It was amazing how quickly we arrived into the heart of the city. We drove around in search of a parking spot. We eventually pulled into a parking garage .

We agreed to walk around and explore a little before dinner, seeing as no one was hungry yet. As we strolled, I took everything in—from the people to the small shops. The shops were high-end.

I never shop at these type of stores.

Darren stopped at a Diesel store and eyed the window display. I followed his gaze to a denim jacket. After a few seconds, he turned to Dad and asked, "Can I go in?"

"Sure, I don't see why not," Dad said. Darren grinned and walked off into the store with Ty on his tail. Dad shortly followed.

I peered into the store and didn't see anything of interest. I was about to head in anyway, but then noticed Mom seemed to have no interest in it either.

"Want to keep walking?" Mom asked.

"How would the boys know where we went?" I inquired, answering her question with another question.

"I'll send your father a text," Mom said. That seemed like a reasonable idea to me.

"Okay," I said.

Mom and I started walking again. As we moved, I strayed off in thought.

I can't believe how much fun I had today. I love when I get to spend time with my family with no distractions. No parents on phone calls, no friends to pull my brother's attention away, and not a single thought about Incognito. Just us as a family. Times like this are few and far between for us, but I cherish them.

I was snapped out of my thoughts when I noticed Mom wasn't by my side anymore. I stopped and turned around to find her looking into a store. I took a few steps back to her.

"Want to go in?" Mom asked me.

"Sure, why not?" I said, not caring one way or the other. I held the door open for my mom as she stepped in. I hadn't been paying any attention to what store we were walking into, but once inside, it didn't take a rocket scientist to figure out it was a Coach store.

I slowly perused the store, looking at all the expensive purses. Nothing caught my attention. It only took one glance around the store to find Mom, since it wasn't a very large space. I walked over to as she was eyeing a big navy purse.

"What do you think?" Mom asked me.

"It…looks great," I said, not knowing what to say.

Mom chuckled, "If you don't like it, you could just say so."

"It's not that I don't like it. You're just asking the wrong person. Do you think I know whether a purse looks good or not?" I said, trying to explain my previous answer.

"You don't have to know anything about purses. I'm just asking if you like the look of it," Mom said, further explaining what exactly she was trying to ask.

"Oh, yeah, it looks nice," I responded.

"Did you see anything you like for yourself?" Mom asked.

I looked around the store. "Not really."

"Alright, I'll go check out then." Mom headed towards the cashier.

I walked toward the store entrance and continued to glance around at all the purses and wallets. Before long, Mom had finished checking out and was by my side.

"Ready?" she asked.

"Yep," I said.

We exited the store to see the boys walking toward us. They must have just finished up in their shop right before we finished up in ours.

"Everyone ready to go find somewhere to eat?" Dad asked.

"I'm ready," Ty replied.

"I'm starving," Darren said, giving his usual response in regards to food.

Mom gave a nod, and I said a simple, "Yep."

"Alright, I asked the cashier when we checked out if he knew of any good restaurants around here, and he told me about an Italian restaurant he likes that's just around the corner. Want to try it out?" Dad asked.

After it was apparent that no one had any objection, we went in search of the restaurant. We followed Dad until he stopped in front of a restaurant with a small outside patio and red awning over the door.

"Here we are," Dad announced.

Dad held the door open for all of us to enter. As soon as I stepped inside, I was overwhelmed by an aroma of food. I wasn't sure what dish the smell was coming from, but it smelled heavenly.

A hostess in an all-black dress greeted us instantly. I suddenly looked down at my outfit of jeans and a T-shirt and felt underdressed. I glanced around at some of the people seated and noticed that we weren't the only ones underdressed for the restaurant. Apparently, other people had been enjoying the shops just like we had and found this restaurant.

I was spending so much attention on how people were dressed that I hadn't noticed Dad had told them how many people. The hostess brought me from my thoughts when she said, "Follow me to your table." Apparently, there wasn't a wait. I was surprised, considering the place was pretty packed.

As I walked to our table, I took in more off my surroundings. I noticed that the lights were slightly dimmed and the walls were a brownish gold with stucco smoothed around to give them texture. The chatter of people in conversations filled the restaurant.

We reached our table, and the hostess set our menus down. "I hope you enjoy your meal," she said before disappearing back to the front of the restaurant. It didn't take long for our waiter to show up and ask us what we wanted to drink. Once the waiter left, I started looking over my menu. There were a lot of choices, so it wasn't an easy decision to make.

The waiter came back with our drinks and bread. "Are you ready for me to take your order, or would you like a few more minutes?" he asked.

"I'm ready. Are you guys?" Dad asked, directing his question at Darren, Ty, and me. We all knew Mom would be ready. She wasn't an indecisive person. She could make up her mind on the spot about anything—business, food, clothes, anything, you name it—she could make a quick decision.

I wish I were as sure of my choices as she is instead of second guessing everything I ever think.

"I'm ready," Darren said, answering Dad's question.

"Me too," Ty chimed in.

"I'll be ready," I said. The waiter started with Mom's order, then Darren's, then Dad's, then Ty's, and finally mine. I figured out what I wanted while Mom and Darren were ordering. I gave my order, and the waiter disappeared to put our order in.

Mom was the first to break the silence. "What do you guys think of the city?" she asked. Before Darren or I could say a word, Ty was already answering her question—no surprise there. He was talking a mile a minute, and surprisingly we could make out everything he was saying. His eyes shone with awe and amazement.

Sometimes I wish I was young again to see everything in such an exciting way. I love to hear Ty explain his experiences. You would think it was the best thing ever, and yet I guarantee he would beat the experience within a day. Ty can make the most ordinary event seem like it had been the event of the year.

I listened to him talk until he was finished. I thought, *for once I won't be last to give my opinion*—but right as I was about to speak up, Darren started talking. I wasn't brave enough or loud enough to try and fight to be heard over Darren.

I can't help it. Both of my brothers were born for the spotlight, and I was designed to be in their shadows—which isn't bad all the time. Sometimes I just wish I was as entertaining as they are.

I pulled myself out of my thoughts and started listening to Darren's description of the town. Darren described it entirely differently then Ty had. Darren didn't have the same wonder in his eyes, but he still held attention. Darren wasn't a man of many words, yet somehow he was a fantastic storyteller. He always found a way to weave humor into any story.

It's funny the differences between what the two boys paid attention to about the city. The boys may look alike, but they don't think alike.

I hadn't noticed that Darren had finished talking until Dad asked me, "What about you?" I was quickly snapped out of my daze but wasn't sure what he was asking me about, because I wasn't paying attention to the conversation at that moment.

"What about me?" I asked, responding to his question with another question.

"What did you think of the city?" Dad clarified his question.

"Oh, I think it's quite beautiful. I love all the intricate architecture, and it's fun just to walk around and people watch," I said, finishing my much shorter description than the boys.

"That's it? That's boring," Darren said, clearly not intrigued by my short description.

I sighed. "Well, I'm sorry I'm not as interesting as you and Ty," I said with spite.

I focused my attention on fiddling with my napkin on my lap. Before anyone could respond to my outburst, the waiter showed up with our food. As he sat my plate of fettuccine alfredo in front of me, I smiled at the delightful aroma coming from it.

I watched as Ty bounced up and down in his seat when the waiter placed his lasagna in front of him, and I saw a small smile spread across Darren's lips at the sight of his seafood pasta. Mom and Dad both gave polite smiles and thanked the waiter as he set their various chicken dishes down. The waiter made sure we didn't need anything else and then departed.

The rest of dinner was relatively uneventful. No one addressed my outburst. We just continued with dinner like it had never happened. I wasn't sure if I was glad that no one brought it up or a little hurt that no one cared enough to mention it.

It dawned on me how ridiculous I was being. *It's not a competition between siblings. I should just be enjoying our family time.*

We finished our meal and waited for the check. I drifted in and out of the conversation; I was too distracted by my thoughts to be a true part of the discussion. The same thought kept ringing in my head: *It isn't a competition. I've always seen it as a competition.*

Chapter 28

We exited the restaurant and Mom said, "It's time we should head back to the car." No one argued against Mom's decision, so we started our walk.

I fell off in my thoughts again. *I've always thought about my relationship with my brothers like it was a competition. I've tried to be as good as they are. I've wanted to be as entertaining as they are. I've never thought I measured up; but that's the problem, isn't it? I'm not supposed to be my brothers—or be as good as they are. Being siblings isn't a competition of who is better. I'm not them, and I can't be like them. I was designed to be the way I am, flaws and all. My brothers aren't my competition. They're my friends. I don't get to choose my family, but I can choose how I view my family.*

I was yanked from my thoughts once again when I noticed someone fell into step next to me without a word. I peered over and saw Darren.

"Look, I—" I said.

At the same time, Darren spoke. "Kinsley, listen—." We both chuckled. Darren continued, "Please, let me finish what I was going to say. First, I'm sorry. I didn't mean to offend you with what I said. I meant it as a joke—not a very funny one—but a joke nonetheless." I tried to keep eye contact with Darren while he spoke, but his gaze remained focused on the concrete, except for periodic glances at me. His shoulders slumped down slightly.

I wasn't used to seeing this side of Darren. He had insulted me many times before and not noticed what he had done, yet I could tell this time he regretted what he had said. I wanted to ask him what had changed, but I wasn't sure he would even know. All I knew was that I saw my brother through new eyes. He was learning, slowly—very, very slowly—but he was, and that spoke volumes about his character.

"Darren, thank you for apologizing. It means a lot. I was wrong too though. My outburst wasn't an okay response," I said sincerely. Darren started to interrupt me, but for once I had enough courage to stop him. "I'm not finished yet. I let you finish. Now let me finish."

Darren nodded, showing me he understood. I shifted my gaze to the concrete before hesitantly saying, "The reason your comment hurt was because I know I can't measure up to you and Ty—not in talent, not in storytelling, not in anything." Darren opened his mouth to speak, but then closed it when I gave him a warning look, signaling I still wasn't finished. I continued, "But I realized that's okay. I'm not you. I'm going to be very different from you and Ty, and that's okay. So if I'm boring, so be it."

I moved my eyes from the concrete to where Darren had been, but he wasn't there. I stopped walking and turned around. Darren stood frozen several strides behind me, staring at me in disbelief. I walked back to him. "Are you okay?" I asked, as I scanned my brother's face, looking for signs of anger. I couldn't read him.

"That...That's what you think I think of you?" he asked, almost struggling to get the words out.

I shrugged and looked at the ground. "Isn't that what everyone thinks of me?" I said, unable to get myself to look him in the eye.

"I have never once thought you were boring. Now, on multiple occasions, I've thought you were annoying—but never boring." He tried to bring some humor to the situation. I gave a slight chuckle. Darren continued, "I've always thought you are one of *the most interesting people I know* ." You are the one person I've never been able to figure out, and you're my sister. Your talents, your interests—it's like you hold your cards close to your chest and slowly reveal them, one at a time, just to wow people more than if you'd shown them all at once. Kinsley, I've never seen you as not measuring up. If anything, I always thought you set the bar of what I had to reach."

After Darren finished, I tried to process everything he'd said. *I had no idea he thought of me this way. All this time, when I felt I had to measure up to him, he thought he had to measure up to me.*

"Wow...aren't we a messed up bunch?" I said, only half joking.

Darren laughed. "No kidding," he agreed.

"Darren, thank you. I had no idea you saw me that way. I mean, I see you as just as incredible as you see me."

"Then I guess that makes us even," Darren said with a smile.

"I guess it does," I said, smiling back at him.

Just then I was broken from our bonding moment by hearing Dad yell at the end of the block: "Kinsley, Darren—come on!"

We looked at each other. "Race, yeah?" Darren announced as he took off running. I instinctively sprinted after him, weaving in and out of the people who were strolling on the busy sidewalk. It was difficult to run after Darren when I was trying not to collide with a light pole or person. To no surprise, Darren beat me to the corner.

Once I got there, Darren was wearing his signature smirk. "I won," he boasted.

I rolled my eyes. "Yes, that's apparent. Thank you, Captain Obvious."

"What were you guys doing way back there?" Dad asked, his eyebrows furrowed, probably from both confusion and irritation.

I looked at Darren and smiled. "Admiring the uniqueness of it all," I said, knowing that Darren knew I was talking about more than just the city.

"Okay, come on. Let's catch up to the other two," Dad said before starting to walk again.

I became lost in my head on the way back to the hotel. *I never knew Darren saw me as the person to beat, and I never realized I saw my siblings as competition. I guess this trip has opened my eyes to some things.*

Back at the hotel, everyone was tired and ready to head to bed. I said goodnight and went into my room. I got ready for bed and laid down—excited for what the next day might bring.

Chapter 29

I woke up in the morning with no alarm needed, rolled onto my side, and looked at the clock on the side table. 7 a.m.—I debated whether I should get ready for the day or just hang out in my PJs for a while.

I decided to go out to the family room area, see who was up, and go from there. I saw that only my dad was there and did a double take just to make sure I hadn't seen wrong.

"Are you the only one up?" I questioned.

My dad looked up from his computer. "Yep. Well, not exactly. Mom's up. She's in our room getting ready," Dad said.

That made more sense. Dad and Mom both typically woke up early. I would be shocked if Dad were the only one awake.

"Ah, that makes sense," I said, making my way over to the couch and flopping down. I looked at my phone, and to no surprise, had no text messages. *Who would want to talk to me anyway?*

I was about to go on Instagram when Dad continued the conversation. "Any thoughts about what you want to do today?" he asked.

I thought for a moment. "No, not really," I said, pausing slightly before I continued, "What about you?"

Dad was hesitant to answer my question. "I wondered if your mother would enjoy a day at the spa and a dinner date, but I don't want to leave you guys alone on what's supposed to be a family vacation."

"She would love that! You two don't get a lot of date nights, and she rarely gets to the spa," I said with a genuinely happy tone.

"But what about you guys? It doesn't feel right leaving you alone all day." Concern laced Dad's voice.

I smiled. *Always the protective father, making sure his kids are fine before thinking about himself.*

"You guys deserve a day to yourselves. Besides, we'll be fine." Before I continued, Dad looked at me, raising his eyebrow. I knew what he was thinking. "...Okay, I will make sure the boys don't do anything stupid," I said.

Dad chuckled. "That seems more accurate. Are you sure you're OK with this? I know how badly you were looking forward to our family time," Dad said.

I gave my dad a warm smile. "You're right. I was looking forward to family time, I've had a blast so far, and there's always tomorrow. You guys hardly ever take any time for your selves. You guys need this," I responded, with my eyes locked with Dad's.

"Alright, you twisted my arm," Dad said, finally giving in.

I smiled victoriously and threw my arms up. "Yes! I win." Dad just smiled and shook his head at my antics.

Mom came out all dressed and ready for the day. She even had her shoes on.

That's typical of Mom, always one step ahead of the rest of us.

"Anyone hungry yet?" Mom asked.

"I am," I replied.

"Alright, you two get ready for breakfast, and I'll go wake the boys," Mom ordered before heading off into the boys' room, not wasting any time.

Dad looked at the space where Mom previously was and mock saluted. "On it, captain!" I laughed, knowing all too well he was only brave enough to do that because Mom was out of earshot.

Upon entering my room to get ready, a small smile spread across my lips at the thought that if we were eating at the cafe here, I might see Advanced Company. *Wait. Is it weird if I see them when I'm with my family? I'm sure Darren would find some way to tease me about it.* My smile fell. *I hope we're eating out somewhere. I don't want Darren to embarrass me.*

When I reentered the family room, Dad came out the same time as I did.

"We're just waiting for the boys," Mom informed us.

I feigned being shocked. "Really? What a surprise." The boys were always the last ones ready. I guess my family broke the whole cliche about girls taking forever and guys constantly having to wait for the girls.

Shortly, the boys emerged from their room. "Alright, let's go," Dad said as he grabbed the car keys and we headed for the elevator.

As we passed the dining area, I was happy we were eating elsewhere. I didn't want the potential embarrassment of my family meeting Advanced Company. I gave into my urge to glance over to see if Advanced Company was there, but they weren't. For some reason, I was a little bummed. I ignored the feeling as I followed my family out the door.

After about 20 minutes of driving, we pulled into the parking lot of a breakfast joint. I stepped inside, and I was surprised. The restaurant was tiny and packed inside but used its space well. I glanced around the small establishment. It had no real theme evident—just a small breakfast joint that I hoped had good food.

Dad walked back from putting our name in. "Should be only 20 to 25 minutes," he said.

"How did you find this place?" I asked Dad, surprised that he would know about such a hole-in-the-wall establishment.

"Someone from the showcase who lives in the area recommended it. He said it was the best breakfast joint nearby." I smiled, leave it to Dad to learn about a breakfast joint from a total stranger. It fell in line with his two favorite things: breakfast and people.

I was shocked when the hostess called our name and escorted us to our table. The wait had been much shorter than 20 minutes. I perused the menu and quickly decided what I wanted. Breakfast was the one meal that was an easy decision for me.

The waitress appeared and asked for our drink order. I was surprised when she didn't bother writing it down. *I guess she has a good memory.* Everyone looked quietly over the menu. Judging by Ty's grimace, I knew the only reason he wasn't his talkative self was because it was still too early for him.

The waitress was quick to return with the drinks, not getting a single one wrong despite not writing it down.

"Are you all ready to order?" she asked. Darren and I nodded to signal we had made up our minds, Dad gave a simple yes. No one needed to bother to ask mom, and Ty was the only one who hadn't given a response.

Dad asked Ty, "Do you know what you want?"

Ty looked up from his menu. "Yep."

My Dad looked at the waitress. "We are good to go," Dad said. The waitress smiled and pulled out her pad and pen to take our orders. I listened as Mom ordered some veggie omelet with hash browns; Darren ordered a large breakfast plate with eggs, various sides of meat, home-fries, and toast; and Dad got a meat lover's omelet coupled with hash browns and toast.

The waitress looked at me to signal she was ready for my order.

"I'll have eggs and bacon," I said.

"Hash-browns or home-fries?" she asked. I shook my head. "Neither." The waitress lowered her pad and gave me a slight quizzical look.

"Toast or pancakes?"

I gave her a sheepish smile and said, "None." She was polite and didn't say anything else, but I could tell she thought my order was strange. My family, on the other hand, didn't bat an eye. *They're used to my boring order.*

She took Ty's order, which was French toast, and then she left.

No one spoke for a minute. It dawned on me that I was the only one Dad had told about his plans for the day. Since Dad was sitting beside me, I was able to nudge him, hoping he would get the idea. He just looked at me and raised his eyebrows. I knew he wasn't going to get what I was trying to say.

"Dad had an idea for today," I said, hoping he would catch on and continue.

"Oh yeah," Dad said. He looked at Mom. "I thought maybe you would enjoy a spa day, and then we could have a dinner date tonight."

Mom took a second before she responded. "What made you think of this? And wouldn't that mean the kids would be left alone all day?" Mom asked, her eyes darting to me and then back to my dad.

I find it funny. One minute, they couldn't care less what I was doing while the showcase was going on; but now all of a sudden they're worried about me. I don't get parents; but then again, Mom always says I'll understand if I ever have kids of my own.

Before Dad could answer, I spoke up. I knew Dad wasn't enough to convince her. I knew her only hesitation was because I was so excited for family time.

"I already told Dad it was okay—"

I was quickly cut off by Darren. "Why don't we get a say in this?" he cut in, motioning between Ty and himself. I rolled my eyes but continued ignoring Darren's comment.

"I thought you guys deserved some alone time, and it would also give us some sibling bonding time," I said to Mom with a smile.

I was fully expecting Darren to object or make some joke, but for once he kept his mouth shut. My mom scanned my face, probably looking for any sign that I was lying. She then looked back to Dad. "If the kids are all okay with it, then I would love to," she said, laying out her condition. Her answer was less business-woman and more loving wife and mother.

Dad looked at Darren and Ty but didn't have to ask anything. Darren already knew what he was going to ask. "I don't mind the lack of parental supervision today," he said with a devious smirk.

I shook my head. "You may not have parent supervision, but you have sister supervision," I said, smirking back.

"That doesn't make any sense. I'm older than you. I should be the one in charge," Darren objected.

I didn't use my classic comeback where I say I'm *more mature;* I used a more clever response this time. "Well, which one of us is more likely to catch something on fire or get themselves hurt?" I raised my eyebrows and shot a knowing smirk.

Darren raised a finger toward me. "That? Yeah, that would be me," he said, lowering his finger in surrender.

Darren and I smiled, knowing how true that statement was.

Dad smiled and shook his head at our exchange.

Just then, the waitress came back with our food. She deposited our food, gave me one last glance, and then walked away. Once she had left the table, Dad looked at Ty,

"What about you, Ty? Are you okay just hanging out with Darren and Kinsley today?" Dad asked.

We all looked at Ty. I was ready to try persuading him that we could have just as much fun without Mom and Dad.

"Can I pick the first thing we do?" Ty questioned, shifting his eyes to Darren and me. I looked at Darren, and he just shrugged, showing he didn't care.

"Sure, I don't see why not," I responded.

Ty's smile grew. "Yes! Then sure. I don't care," Ty said, his eyes glowing with happiness.

Mom looked at Dad. "Then I guess it's a date!" she said as a smile graced her lips. Dad smiled back with a big goofy grin.

The rest of breakfast, we didn't talk about a whole lot. Everyone was too busy eating. Once we were finished and Dad had paid the check, we all piled back into the rental car and made our way back to the hotel. We weren't in our rooms long before Dad and Mom were ready to leave.

"Okay, guys, we'll see you late tonight—if not when we come back, before we go to dinner," Mom said.

I hugged both my parents. "Have a good time, and don't worry about us. We'll be fine," I said.

After they exited the hotel room, I had no idea what we were going to do all day long. I just hoped I didn't have to play babysitter too much.

I walked back over to the family room, sat in a chair, and looked at my brothers on the couch. They were both on their phones and didn't say anything. I waited a minute before I spoke up. "So Ty, what is it you wanted to do?" I inquired. *I know he has something in mind,* I thought.

Ty's eyes darted up from his phone and met mine. He had a big grin on his face. "I want to go to the arcade!" The excitement was evident in his voice and from the fact he could no longer sit still.

Darren looked up from his phone but didn't say anything. "Well, what are we waiting for? Let's go!" I said as I stood up from the chair. Ty nearly leaped off the couch and ran to the door.

Darren sighed as he stood up. "Why did we let him choose the first thing?" he asked as we walked to the door. Ty opened it in a flash and disappeared down the hall.

I tilted my head and gave Darren a "mom look," as Darren had labeled it. "You can drop your cool act," I said, using my fingers to put quotes around *cool.* "You and I both know you are almost as excited as he is."

After I finished, a small smile played on Darren's lips. "First, I don't have a cool act. I just am cool." I rolled my eyes at Darren, even though he probably didn't notice. "And secondly, arcades are for children, not adults."

I looked at Darren as we waited for the elevator. "First, you're not that cool," I said. "And second, you know Dad would be just as excited as Ty."

I could tell Darren was about to reject my point, but then once he thought about it, reluctantly said, "Yeah, okay, you win."

I smirked at Darren as we entered the empty elevator. "You said I win, that means you admit you are excited."

Darren smiled slightly, keeping his gaze on the elevator doors. "Maybe a little," he said. I didn't say anything else—just kept smiling as the elevator dropped toward the lobby floor.

Darren and Ty weren't the only ones excited.

Chapter 30

As we entered the arcade, I was mildly surprised and very grateful that it wasn't crowded. There were decent numbers of kids, but it wasn't like it was packed with kids running around everywhere.

I looked at Ty, ready to ask him what he wanted to do first, when I saw he had already walked off toward a game. I followed Ty to make sure I didn't lose him. I was surprised at how big the arcade was. I caught up with Ty at the game of his choice, when Darren showed up with a significant number of tokens for the games.

Ty finished his game, and before I could ask what we were doing next, Darren had already walked off toward another game. Ty and I caught up to Darren when he stopped at none other than a shooting machine. The game had only two guns. Two guns meant two players.

Ty picked up the second gun, and I was left standing there. *Good thing I didn't want to play,* I thought.

I watched as Darren explained the game to Ty. *They may be years apart and nothing alike, but that doesn't seem to matter to them. Darren has always been such a good older brother to Ty, and Ty has always looked up to Darren and loved being around him. They have a special bond with each other—a bond I'll never have.* Their close bond only fed my exclusion.

I watched my brothers get so involved in the game that they didn't have a clue about their surroundings. Ty and Darren both started talking to each other, excitedly gaming. Various "dies," "nos," and anything else you could think of spouted from the two. *I could leave, and they wouldn't even notice.*

I patiently waited for them to finish, and before I could say a word, the boys were already on the hunt for the next game. *Do they even know I exist?* I chased after them.

For a while, we roamed the arcade, the boys taking turns playing games. I played here and there, but not a lot. It's not that I didn't enjoy arcades; I liked them a lot. I didn't like the games the boys were picking, and I wasn't courageous enough to suggest a different game. *Some battles really aren't worth it.*

I just had gotten used to the fact that Darren and Ty together overruled me and that I'd be sitting out most of the games—when we came to a mock racing game. Once again, it was a two-player game. *Yay, another game I get to sit out...*

I assumed Ty would want to play with Darren, but he didn't say anything. Instead, he walked over by the chair Darren sat in and watched his screen. It hadn't registered to me yet that he didn't want to play.

Darren looked over at me. "Are you playing or leaving me by myself?" he asked.

My eyebrows raised. "Oh, I get to play this one?" The boys either ignored me or were too enamored by the game to hear what I'd said. I crossed over and slumped down in the chair next to Darren. I was terrible at racing games, and I didn't think they were that fun to play. Every time, I'd either crash or come in last. *However, I'll take what I can get.*

The boys had just started playing their next game that was two-player, go figure. *I wonder if Advanced Company is having more fun than I am.* I ignored the thought and tried to focus on the fact that it was just a blessing that I was getting time with my brothers.

I took a moment to look around at the other kids playing, when one game caught my attention. It was the one I'd been looking for but hadn't found yet—skeeball.

The boys finished their game, and before I could be dragged off to another game, I spoke up. "My turn to decide," I said. Ty opened his mouth in protest, but I cut him off. "I haven't chosen a single game. I'm picking the next one." I wasn't leaving room for arguments. *I have been dragged around this arcade all afternoon. I can pick one game without it being considered selfish, right?*

Ty let out a heavy sigh. "Fine," was all Ty said. Darren just raised his eyebrows as if to ask, what game? I waved for them to follow me and walked over to the row of skeeball machines. I put my coins in one, and it started up. I looked over and found the boys doing the same thing.

The boys finished at about the same time as I did.

"I want to play one more round," I announced.

"Okay," Darren said as he stepped behind me to watch. I inserted my coins and started playing again. I finished and turned around to talk to Darren, only to find the spot he and Ty had previously occupied was empty.

I glanced around in hopes they were close by, but of course, I had no luck. I figured I would text Darren and ask where they were. When I reached into my pocket for my phone, I quickly realized that I'd left it upstairs. I groaned. *Great, now what am I supposed to do?*

Chapter 31

I searched through the arcade, looking all around and listening for any sign of my brothers. The arcade was too loud to hear their voices. *Why am I even looking for them? It's not like they'll have even noticed I'm gone.* I was jolted from my thoughts when I ran into someone.

The person quickly reached out and grabbed my arms to steady me before I fell over. I looked at him for the first time to apologize, when I saw a very familiar pair of eyes staring back at me.

"We've got to stop meeting like this," Justin said as he released my arms.

I gave a short laugh. "Yeah, no kidding."

"You know, if I didn't know any better, I would say you're doing it on purpose." I opened my mouth to protest when Justin continued, "But I know you're just that clumsy." Justin smirked and chuckled at my offended expression and gaping mouth.

"I am not clumsy," I protested.

"Yeah, that's why you've run into me twice," Justin said playfully.

I shook my head. "I remember the first was both of our faults, and running into you doesn't make me clumsy. I just wasn't paying attention to where I was going," I said, defending myself.

"Yeah, you seemed like you were looking for someone," Justin stated.

My eyes widened in realization."You knew I was going to run into you?"

Justin shrugged with a smirk. "Maybe," he said.

I gave his arm a playful hit. "Dork," I said.

He chuckled. "Was that suppose to hurt?"

"No, it wasn't," I replied with a smile.

The rest of Advanced Company walked over from one of the arcade games.

"Fancy meeting you here," Nick said.

"What are you doing here?" Tommy asked.

"Well, I was supposed to be here with my brothers, but I seem to have lost them," I said, glancing around.

"We would offer to help you find them, but we have no idea what they look like," Adam said.

I focused back on the group. "Oh, that's not necessary. I'm sure I'll find them eventually." *It's not like my brothers miss me.* "Well, I've kept you boys from your games long enough."

None of the boys went to move.

"Why don't you join us?" Tommy offered. I smiled, not surprised that he would offer that.

I was about to object when Justin spoke up. "And do not say you don't want to be a bother; you're not. Besides, I'm sure we'll slowly make our way through the arcade. Maybe we'll run into your brothers." Justin met my gaze. I quickly scanned each boy's face for any sign that they didn't want me to tag along, but I couldn't find any.

I quickly debated their offer. *Following them around can't be any worse than following my brothers around. They claim I'm not a bother, and I usually have a good time with them. So... What could it hurt?*

"Sounds like a plan," I said, smiling back at Justin.

"Shall the beautiful lady decide where we go next?" Nick said, bowing. He was trying to be charming but just ended up looking like a dork instead.

I laughed. "Nice try, but flattery will get you nowhere. And no—that honor falls on someone else."

Tommy pointed toward a game. "What about that one?" he said. None of the boys objected. Tommy led us over to the machine.

I watched as the boys took turns playing, all intently watching the other players.

Justin leaned over to me and talked quietly enough so the others couldn't hear. "It's only flattery if it's not true," he said. I felt the heat slowly rise on my cheeks as I looked at the ground, not sure how to respond to his remark.

The boys finished their game, and we headed to the next one. It felt kind of like following my brothers around, only for some reason I enjoyed it more. When a boy wasn't playing, he would end up in a conversation with me. They alternated which guy talked to me with each game. *I feel more included with them than with my brothers.*

We were walking to the next game, when Justin and Nick stopped. I was the first to notice. "Hey, guys," I said, calling after Adam and Tommy. The two boys came back to where Nick and Justin were standing. They were both looking at one of the games involving shooting hoops. Adam looked at them and then back to me with raised eyebrows. I just shrugged in response, not knowing what they were thinking.

Nick and Justin suddenly looked at each other. "You thinking what I'm thinking?" Nick asked Justin.

"Yeah, that I'm going to kick your butt," Justin said with a smirk.

Nick crossed his arms. "I believe I won last time we played basketball," Nick said with arrogance.

Justin nodded slowly before saying, "That may be true, but I let you win." Nick scoffed, then Justin continued, "We both know I'm better at shooting straight-on shots than you are." Justin finished with his arms crossed, mimicking Nick.

I spoke to Adam, not taking my eyes off the two boys standing face to face. "Are they always this competitive?"

"You have no idea," Adam said with his eyes locked on the two boys.

Just as Nick and Justin were about to insert their coins, Adam spoke up. "You never asked if any of us wanted to join this little competition."

Adam had gotten their attention. Both boys turned around to face Tommy, Adam, and me. "We just assumed you didn't, because you and Tommy don't usually like to participate in our one-on-one competitions," Nick said, explaining his actions.

Adam sighed. "Tommy and I aren't the only people here," he said, gesturing toward me.

I quickly looked at Adam with wide eyes. I didn't want to be put in the middle of this. I don't do well with conflict.

"You play?" Justin asked, trying to hide his surprise.

"No, I don't play. However, I do like this game," I mumbled, fiddling with my hands. Nick looked at the other two machines next to the ones they had chosen.

"Well, there are two more machines. If the two of you are brave enough to compete, go for it," Nick said with a raised eyebrow and a confident stance.

I don't know if I should play or not. I like this game, but I don't want to make a fool out of myself. But then again, I'm tired of being pulled around an arcade all day while hardly playing anything.

I was pulled from my thoughts when Tommy's hand quickly shot into the air. "I want to play, but not for competition. Just for fun," Tommy said, looking at me.

"Why are you looking at me?" I asked in surprise.

"I want you to play. For fun," Tommy said with pleading eyes. When I was slow to answer, Tommy continued pleading. "Please."

I don't know if it was a lapse of judgment or Tommy's pleading eyes, but I caved. "Fine. I'll play."

Chapter 32

Tommy and I strode over to the other two machines. I put my coins in and began the game. I picked up the first basketball and shot it straight into the basket. I just kept picking up ball after ball. As I threw one of my balls that was set to go straight into the hoop, another ball suddenly knocked it off course. I was stunned for a minute and looked over to find a laughing Tommy,

"That's not very fair," I said, feigning annoyance that he'd set my ball off course.

Tommy smiled and continued shooting hoops. I grabbed one of my basketballs and did the same thing he'd done to me. Adam, Tommy, and I burst out laughing.

"You know that defeats the purpose of the game. You're supposed to stick to your own hoop," Adam said with a amusement in his voice.

"Where's the fun in that?" I asked as I went back to shooting hoops.

We kept shooting until the game was over. Tommy looked at his score and then mine.

"Wow, you destroyed me," he said with slight awe.

Before I could say anything, a pouting Nick and a smug Justin came over. That answered who'd won between them.

"How'd it go?" Justin asked.

Before I could say anything, Adam spoke. "See for yourself." He gestured toward my machine that still had my score displayed. Both Nick and Justin looked at the screen.

The smile instantly dropped from Justin's face. It was like sticking a pin in a balloon. I looked at Adam and Tommy and saw they were enjoying this as much as I was.

"How did you guys do?" I asked, with as sweet a tone and face as I could manage.

Justin and Nick didn't say anything for a second. Justin was the first to regain his composure.

"Oh, that doesn't matter. What matters is we had fun. Right, guys?" Justin said, looking at Tommy and Adam for help.

"I beat you, didn't I?" I said, crossing my arms.

Justin rubbed the back of his neck. "Well… I mean, you…" Justin stuttered.

"Use your words."

"Fine, you won," Justin said, looking at the ground.

I smiled victoriously, knowing it wasn't easy for either boy to admit defeat. I waved my hand as though I were waving the matter off.

"Beginners luck, I'm sure," I said, as I shared a smile with Adam and Tommy.

Justin and Nick had both fully regained their composure and had picked up what was left of their pride. "Where to?" Nick asked.

"I could go for a snack," Adam said. All of the boys agreed.

We made our way over to the snack bar, and the boys ordered what they wanted. Justin looked at me. "Do you want anything?" he asked.

I shook my head. "Um… just some water," I said. Justin nodded and turned back around to the counter.

I saw Tommy had picked a table, and I walked over and joined him. The other boys soon came over, and Justin sat my water down in front of me.

"Thank you," I said.

"No problem," Justin replied. The boy's order was quickly called, and Justin and Nick got up to retrieve their order of cheese-smothered nachos and soda from the pickup window.

The boys returned with the food and sat back down.

"I'm glad we ran into you," Tommy said, giving me a warm smile.

"I'm glad I ran into you guys as well," I returned the smile.

I then shifted my attention to Adam. "I mean, someone had to put those two in their place." I finished gesturing toward Nick and Justin, who both had their mouths open, about to protest.

Adam spoke up before they could. "Guess you guys aren't quite as good as you think you are."

Justin sighed, finally giving in. "You are correct. Kinsley is better at shooting hoops than we are," Justin said without a sign of sarcasm in his body language or tone. Justin then shifted his gaze from Adam toward me. "You are quite impressive." *Impressive. He just called me impressive. Is he only referring to my basketball skills or…?*

I was trying to determine how to respond to that compliment, when all of a sudden, I saw my brothers walking toward the snack area.

Darren spotted me and pointed me out to Ty, who smiled and walked over to me. As my brothers approached the table all I could think was, *Please don't embarrass me. Please don't embarrass me.*

"Where have you been? We couldn't find you anywhere!" Ty inquired, but then in true Ty fashion, continued too fast for me to answer, "You missed it. Darren and I—"

Darren interrupted Ty. "Slow down; you're talking way too fast. Give her a chance to answer you!" Darren admonished. He then glanced at the table of unknown faces and said, "So, who are you guys?"

I realized my brothers had never met them before. "Oh, right. Darren, Ty—this is Justin, Nick, Adam, and Tommy. Guys—these are my brothers, Ty and Darren." I pointed to each name I mentioned.

"It's nice to meet you all," Darren said

"You as well," Justin responded.

"How do you all know each other?" Darren asked, looking around the table.

"Well, we (Nick spoke and gestured toward Adam, Tommy, and Justin) are in a dance group together: Advanced Company."

Darren gave a slow nod. "You're the group who danced in the showcase," he said, as he mentally put the pieces together.

"That's us," Tommy said.

Ty looked at the group of guys and then me. "How do you guys know my sister?" Darren asked with scrunched eyebrows.

I suddenly didn't know what to say. My relationship with them was complicated in my head. I knew them as both Incognito and myself. Explaining how I met them without giving anything away was hard for me. I could easily slip up and reveal too much.

Lucky for me, Justin spoke up. "I ran into her—literally. Then I introduced her to the rest of the group, and we've continued to run into each other around the hotel some," Justin explained.

"Oh, okay," Darren said. He paused for a minute and then continued, "Well, are you ready to exchange our tickets and get something to eat?" Darren asked me.

"Yeah, you head over. I'm right behind you," I said as I started to get up from the table. Darren and Ty said bye to the table and then headed off to the prize counter.

"See you around?" Justin said, with hopeful eyes.

"I'm sure I'll run into you guys again," I said with a smile, as I walked off to join my brothers at the prize counter.

I walked up to my brothers and set my tickets on the counter. "All yours," I said as I slid the small slips of paper toward my brothers.

Darren looked at me, confused. "You don't want anything?" he asked.

"Nope, I just enjoyed playing the games," I answered.

Darren and Ty shrugged and went back to deciding on their prizes. When the boys had finished picking their prizes, Darren with a football and Ty with a giant rainbow slinky, we walked out of the arcade.

"Where to next?" I questioned. Both boys were quiet for a moment.

"Back to the hotel room to chill and order pizza?" Darren asked. Ty and I liked the sound of that.

Chapter 33

The boys departed to their room to change into more comfortable clothes. I decided to do the same thing and throw on a pair of sweatpants and an oversized T-shirt. I grabbed my phone off my bed, returned to the family room, and sat on the couch.

I opened my messages and quickly typed my parents a text saying, "No injuries, no fires, and now back in the room for the night. Going to order pizza."

Mom quickly responded: "Glad to hear it. See you when we get back from dinner." Darren and Ty came out of their room in similar attire to mine. Ty sat on the couch, and Darren took a chair.

"Do we want to order pizza and then watch a movie?" I asked.

"Sounds good to me," Darren said.

"Yeah!" Ty exclaimed. I asked the boys what they wanted on their pizzas, even though I already knew.

Darren, of course, said meat lovers—and Ty wanted pineapple and pepperoni. I called in the two pizzas. Before long, the pizza arrived. I handed out the food and took my seat on the couch. Now for the hard part.

"What movie are we watching?" I asked. Darren and Ty just shrugged. "You guys are so helpful," I said, my voice laced with sarcasm. I turned the TV on, went to On Demand, and started perusing the movies. It took a while before we could find one that all three of us agreed on.

I was expecting just to sit and enjoy the movie, but Darren, of course, had to make smart aleck comments throughout the entire thing—making us all laugh. It wasn't long before Ty picked up on what he was doing and joined in. I just smiled and laughed at my brothers.

I finally decided I wanted to join in. I said a few remarks that I expected to fall flat, but instead, the boys laughed right along with me. It was the most I had laughed in a long time. The movie came to an end, and Darren stood up.

"Well, it's been real," he said, and before he could continue, I jumped in.

"And it's been fun," I said.

Ty finished. "But it ain't been real fun," Ty smiled.

Darren grinned and shook his head at Ty and me. "You're both ridiculous. I'm going to my room for the night," he said as he walked off. I looked at Ty, knowing all too well what was next.

"Same. Goodnight," Ty said, as he quickly hugged me and ran off to his room.

I wasn't tired yet, so I wasn't about to go to bed. I didn't feel like spending hours staring at a phone screen, so I snatched my headphones, made sure I took my iPhone with me, and headed out the door.

Just as I had let the door close, I realized if Mom and Dad came home and I was gone, they would be worried. I sighed and went back in, quickly scribbled a note saying, "I am wandering the hotel, call if you need me." I exited the room again and made my way to the elevator.

I paused once I stepped out of the elevator. I wasn't sure where I wanted to go or what I wanted to do. I popped my headphones in and turned on my music.

I decided just to wander. I headed for the conference wing to walk around that area of the hotel, since there was likely to be no one there at the time. I mindlessly navigated the halls, turning this way or that, depending on my whims. I eventually found myself face to face with a glass door leading to a courtyard.

I pushed the door open and stepped outside. The sky was already dark, and I couldn't see many stars due to the lights of the resort. I walked farther into the courtyard and saw a large fountain in the center. I marveled at its size and intricate detail; the center column of the fountain where the water trickled down was taller than I was and had three tiers. I sat on the wide concrete edge around the fountain, taking out my headphones and stuffing them back into my pocket.

I glanced around the charming courtyard and saw small hedges lined the perimeter, with trees scattered here and there. A slight breeze graced my skin. The sound of the fountain was soothing, almost lulling me to sleep. I smelled a light, sweet aroma, but I didn't know where it was coming from. I looked around and saw abundant flowers planted around the fountain—no doubt where the glorious scent was coming from.

It was a good thing I didn't find this courtyard sooner, or I would have spent my entire time here missing out on all the great things I'd experienced so far. *This vacation has gone nothing as I thought. In a good way.* I focused back on my surroundings. It was peaceful and calming—something out of a dream.

My dreamy feeling quickly vanished when I heard the very door I had come through open and close. I looked up, startled by the disturbance, and was not surprised one bit by who I saw.

Chapter 34

Even in the dimly lit courtyard, I could tell it was him. Perhaps because I half expected him to show up. It seemed whenever I was alone, he appeared out of thin air.

I'm used to him randomly showing up; it's almost a comfort.

He stayed where he was and took a few minutes before he spoke.

"I promise I'm not following you," he said.

I smiled, not sure if he could even see it due to the dim lighting. Justin hesitated before he continued, "I can…I mean, if I'm bothering you, I could leave." Justin said, searching for the right words while rubbing the back of his neck.

I gave a small lighthearted laugh at him fumbling over his words. He reminded me of myself.

"You're not a bother; I could use the company." I hoped to reassure Justin the intrusion was fine.

I heard him let out a heavy breath before he walked closer. Once he was at the fountain, he gestured next to me.

"May I?" he asked politely. I just smiled and nodded at him to show it was fine. He sat down next to me, making sure to leave an appropriate amount of space.

I went back to listening to the surroundings. I loved to hear the whisper of the wind and trickle of the fountain. We sat in silence for a few minutes. The silence wasn't awkward. It was like two old friends quietly reminiscing. Only we hadn't been friends very long, so I was shocked that he didn't feel the need to start a conversation.

The thought occurred to me, *maybe now is a good time to ask for his phone number so I could stay in touch. Is that weird? Would it be better to ask when the rest of Advanced Company is around and I can ask all of them? That seems like a smarter idea than asking now.*

"How'd you do it?" Justin asked out of nowhere, shaking me from my thoughts. I looked at him with confusion.

"How'd I do what?" I asked, hoping for clarification.

"I mean how'd you beat us at that arcade game if you don't play basketball?"

I laughed. "Really? That's what you're concerned about?" I looked at him like he was crazy.

I'm amused that he's so hung up on this.

"Yes, that is the one thing I want to know. I want to know why I lost," Justin stated, standing his ground.

"It's a secret." I smirked.

Justin's eyes widened in shock, with his mouth slightly agape. "What?? That's not fair," he protested.

I shrugged my shoulders. "Life's not fair."

"That's what you're going with?" he deadpanned.

I nodded my head to signal I wasn't offering any more information. Justin shook his head. "No, you're not going to be let off that easily. How are you good at shooting hoops?" he asked, determination etched on his brow.

"Well, practice makes perfect." I hoped to push his buttons with the vague answer.

"Nope, not good enough," he said, crossing his arms.

Smiling at his almost childish ways, I finally gave in and decided to share my secret. "Fine. Darren, my older brother, used to be in basketball, and my dad would take him to practice shooting hoops. I was often brought along and would shoot baskets at the other end of the court. Anyone—after practicing a lot—can learn how to make a basket."

"I knew it! Beginners luck, my foot! I knew you had to have some basketball experience," he said in a victorious tone.

I scoffed. "I would hardly call shooting hoops basketball experience." I used my fingers to put quotes on *basketball experience*.

Justin laughed, "I just knew someone without practice couldn't beat me," he said with confidence in his voice.

I tilted my head slightly and gave my "really?" look. He laughed at my expression.

We sat in silence a little longer. I slipped my phone out and looked at the time. It was 9 p.m.

"I should be getting back to my room," I stated reluctantly. Justin sighed and stood up.

"Yeah, I should too." He offered his hand to help me up before continuing. "Shall I escort you to your room?" He tried to sound gentlemanly and mature.

I smiled. "You may," I said, taking his hand as I stood up.

He then let go of my hand and gestured in front of him. I took that as a sign to start walking. I headed for the door, and just as I was about to reach for the door handle, Justin grabbed it.

"Ladies first," he said with a charming smile as he opened the door.

I smiled. "Thank you."

"You're welcome," he said politely.

I had noticed that Justin always held the door—especially for girls. I considered that he was gentleman in a world that seemed to be losing sight of what that meant.

As we took our route to the elevator, I let my curiosity get the better of me. "Why do you always hold the door for me or let me go first?" I asked, glancing at him.

He didn't hesitate to answer. "It's a nice thing to do," Justin said before going on to further explain. "I was taught that a man holds the door out of respect for the lady—or anyone else."

I smiled, knowing my brothers were taught the same thing—though they seemed to forget that when it came to their sister.

"Well, it certainly doesn't go unnoticed," I commented before stepping onto the arriving elevator.

We rode it to my floor, and both got off—to my surprise. "You don't have to walk me to my door," I said.

Justin cocked one eyebrow. "And what kind of gentleman would I be if I didn't do that?"

I smiled and shook my head. I didn't see the point in trying to argue when I knew I would lose. We strolled to my door in silence.

"See you around," Justin said.

"See you around," I said. Justin flashed me a final smile before turning around to head back to the elevator.

A smile graced my lips as I headed inside. I saw on the kitchen counter my note had something new written on it: "Let us know once you're back."

I obeyed the directions. I walked to my parents' door and knocked. I heard someone say, "Come in." I entered their room and found my dad sitting on the bed and my mom looking through her suitcase for something.

"I'm back," I announced.

"Thank you for letting us know," Dad said.

"No problem. Goodnight," I said before closing their door.

I got to my room and debated going on Twitter, but I decided it was better just to go straight to bed. As soon as my head hit the pillow, I realized just how tired I was, and I knew sleep would soon be upon me.

Chapter 35

I woke up the day before we had to leave and was sad that it was all going to come to an end. The trip had brought so much fun, the thought of going back to my boring old life kind of sucked. *Oh well, I have to go back to reality eventually,* I thought.

I went to the family room, excited for another family day, but stopped dead in my tracks; no one was there. I assumed everyone was still asleep until I saw a note on the kitchen counter from Mom and Dad that read: "Have an important business meeting. Will be back in the evening. Love you guys."

I sighed. *So much for our last family day. But hey, work is essential. They have to be able to feed us.*

As if on cue, my stomach growled. I scribbled a note to the boys, saying I was going to breakfast.

On my way out, it occurred to me that I could wake up the boys. However, I didn't feel like having anyone snap at me. Neither boy was a morning person. The expression "don't poke the sleeping bear" was accurate for them.

Making my decision, I headed down the hall. When the elevator doors opened, I was half expecting to see Justin or all of Advanced Company, but all I saw was empty space.

After arriving at the dining area and getting my food, I started looking around for a free table but didn't see one. Upon another sweep of the restaurant, I did a double take when I saw a familiar group of people. Go figure; Advanced Company wasn't in the elevator, but they were at breakfast.

Justin noticed me and waved me over. I shot Justin a smile and effortlessly swerved through the maze of tables and chairs to get to their table.

"Hey, guys, how have you been?" I asked, taking the only open seat across from Justin. There were various replies of "good" or "great," but Justin answered with "fantastic." I smiled at Justin's different response.

"Where have you been the past few days? We haven't seen you around much," Adam asked.

"I was hanging with my family. Since the showcase was over, we had some vacation time," I said, explaining my absence.

"That's cool," Adam said.

It was nice getting to hang with them again. We chatted through breakfast. The boys caught me up on what they had done the past few days, and I caught them up on my whereabouts.

Midway through our conversation, I looked up and caught Justin staring at me. His cheeks tinged pink, and he shot me a sheepish smile. I shot a smile back. *Why was he staring at me? Is it because of last night, or does he know something about my secret?* Unfortunately, with the other guys around, I didn't feel comfortable asking him.

We all finished eating and decided we should figure out something to do.

"I hear they have a bowling alley here somewhere," I suggested.

"What hotel has a bowling alley?" Nick asked, pulling a face.

"Apparently this one," I replied.

"I think bowling sounds fun," Tommy said with enthusiasm.

No one objected, so we all started off in search of the bowling alley. It didn't take long to find it. We entered and headed to the shoe rental desk. We all grabbed a set of bowling shoes, then picked out balls.

We walked to the lane they assigned us and set our balls down.

"Who goes first?" Adam asked.

"Ladies first," Justin said without a second thought. The rest of the guys agreed. I didn't particularly want to go first, but since they were all being gentleman, I would have felt bad denying their request.

I grabbed my ball and positioned myself to bowl. *It's been what feels like forever since I've been bowling. It's just like riding a bike, right?* I took a few steps, letting my ball swing back and then come forward to launch from my hand.

I winced when I only managed to knock down two pins.
Apparently a very rusty bike.

"Would you like some pointers?" Nick asked, unable to hide his smirk.

"Like you could do better," I challenged Nick.

"Let the master show you how it's done," Nick said as he stood up. Nick strode toward the bowling balls, as sure of himself as a pro bowler. He proceeded to throw a gutter ball.

The rest of the guys laughed at Nick's defeat, and I just stood there smirking.

"What was that about showing us how it's done?" Justin asked.

"I'm just getting warmed up," Nick said in defense.

"Sure, that's what it is," Justin stated in mock disbelief.

After everyone had bowled, it was clear that Justin was the best bowler out of us. *No surprise there,* I thought. *Justin is good at everything. What's surprising though is he isn't super cocky. He doesn't feel the need to show off or gloat, unlike Nick. He doesn't seem to seek others' approval. It's like he knows who he is and what he's good at and doesn't need anyone to validate him. I wonder what it would take for me to get to that mindset.*

About halfway through the bowling game, I threw yet another gutter ball. I let out an exasperated huff. Everyone else had only gotten better as the game progressed—I managed to get worse. I slumped back down in my chair and crossed my arms.

Justin noticed my unhappy state and tried to cheer me up. "You'll get the hang of it."

"Yeah, probably," I said absentmindedly. What I really wanted to say was, "When? By this time next year? *Why do I have to suck at everything?*"

"Would you like some help?" Justin asked. I read his face for any signs of ridicule, but I could tell his offer was genuine. *I wish I didn't need help in the first place,* I thought.

"I'm okay." *To need someone to teach you how to bowl is embarrassing. I know Justin could probably help me improve, but I don't want to seem like the incompetent girl who can't do anything right. He already saved me from nearly drowning in the wave pool. I don't want him to have to save me here too.*

I was pulled from my thoughts when Justin grabbed my hand and yanked me out of my chair.

"What are you—" I was cut off.

"It's your turn, and I'm going to help you," Justin said. Before I could refuse, he continued, "No, you don't get to argue, and no, you're not a burden. This is something I *want* to do." I nodded my head, speechless.

Justin dropped my hand and proceeded to give me some pointers on the proper way to bowl. A few frames later, Justin had me bowling like a pro. Okay, maybe not a pro, but I was doing gobs better.

Later, everyone grew tired of bowling and decided it was time for a change in scenery.

"What are we gonna do next?" Justin asked as we took off our bowling shoes.

Adam was the first to voice his opinion. "I want some downtime just to hang out and chill," he said.

"That sounds great," I agreed.

"Let's go to the teen lounge," Nick suggested. We all liked the sound of that. As I reached for my bowling ball to return it to its holder, Justin picked it up before I could.

"You know I'm capable of putting my ball back," I said with a smile.

"I never said you couldn't. I'm simply trying to be nice and put it back for you, so you don't have to. It's not because I think you're incapable," Justin said.

"Thank you, for everything. Not just the bowling ball," I said as I fiddled with my hands.

Justin gave me a warm smile. "You're welcome."

We all returned our shoes and left to the lounge. We entered the room, the boys chose a radio station to put on, and we sprawled out in the chairs or on the floor. I sat on the left side of the couch, and Tommy sat on the right. Justin and Adam sat in the two chairs.

I had to hold back a laugh when I looked over to find Nick spread out on the floor, as though he had been shot and had fallen flat on his back.

The music slowly faded into background noise, as my mind became increasingly more active.

I should probably go see what my brothers are doing. However, I did hang out with them yesterday, and I'm enjoying my time with these guys.

It was relaxing to get to do nothing for a moment, until they decided to strike up a conversation about Incognito.

"Justin, have you run into Incognito Moves again?" Nick asked.

Like a rubber band snapping back into place, the boys had my attention. The mention of that name made me tense.

"No, she hasn't been around the past few days," Justin said. I could have sworn when he said that, I saw his eyes dart to me. But I told myself, *no, I'm sure it's all in my head.*

"Maybe she left the hotel?" Tommy asked.

"I don't think so," was all Justin replied.

"It was the coolest thing getting to dance with her!" Tommy said.

"Yeah, I can't believe you got her to say yes, Justin," Adam added his two cents.

"I was honestly surprised myself. However, I don't believe she wanted the showcase to have problems," Justin stated matter-of-factly.

There it was—another dart of his eyes towards me, like he knew a secret no one else did. *I swear I saw it that time. I know I wasn't seeing things. He can't know; he's probably just wanting my input.*

Regardless of what he was thinking, I remained quiet. In fact, I accidentally tuned out the entire conversation. I looked down at my wrist, wishing my bracelet would show up somewhere. I'd never taken it off and didn't have a clue where I'd lost it. It sucked waking up one morning and finding it was gone. I figured I would eventually lose or break the gift, knowing my luck—but it meant the world to me, and I didn't expect to lose it so soon.

I was brought out of my thoughts when I heard one of the guys ask about time. I looked down at my phone, only to realize it was already 5 p.m.

"Well, it was great hanging with you guys, but I should get going," I announced.

"We'll see you tomorrow morning before you leave?" Justin asked, his eyes hopeful.

"Definitely," I said with my eyes locked on Justin's.

Everyone said goodbye, and I left to head back up to my room. As I walked away, I instantly regretted not getting their phone numbers. I had thought about asking but couldn't bring myself actually to do it. I was too much of a chicken.

When I entered the room, I found that my parents were home and everyone was in the family room. They had already made the decision to go out for dinner.

As we sat at dinner, everyone talked about their favorite part of the trip. Ty talked the most. I could tell he'd enjoyed himself. I talked the least—not because I hadn't had fun, but I wasn't sure which part was my favorite.

After dinner, we returned to the hotel. I decided to pack the majority of my stuff that night to make the next morning easier. As I packed, I reflected on the trip. My thoughts wandered.

It was much better than I expected it to be. I suppose I partially owe that to Advanced Company. If I hadn't met them, this trip would have turned out entirely differently; it's weird to think that a bunch of strangers made my stay more enjoyable. I didn't even know them, and yet I spent the majority of my time with them. I mean, I even trusted them enough to perform with their group. Why did I feel so comfortable around them? Why am I slightly sad at the thought of never seeing them again? I guess the answer to those questions is that I made four friends on this trip. Despite my initial reluctance, they managed to charm their way into being my friends. Who am I kidding? They didn't charm anyone. They were genuine, kind, and real; it would have been hard not to get along with them—hard not to get along with Justin.

I finished packing and decided to go to bed, because I had an early morning. I laid down and couldn't help but wonder if they would miss me too. Familiar thoughts passed through my mind as I drifted to sleep...

Probably not. The boys are on the rise to becoming famous; I am a nobody. I bet they will remember Incognito though. She's unforgettable. Me, on the other hand—that's another story.

<h1 style="text-align:center">Chapter 36</h1>

In the morning, I prepared for the long trip home. I finished packing what little bit of stuff I had remaining. Once out of my room, I saw that my family was packed and ready to go.

"Everyone ready?" Dad asked. We all either nodded or responded with a yes. We grabbed our bags and headed to the elevators.

In the elevator, I got my first good look of the day at Ty and Darren. Ty looked like a zombie, and Darren looked like he was sleepwalking. When we got to the lobby, Dad went to the front desk to return our key cards and check us out. I glanced around the lobby, hoping I would see Advanced Company before I left.

Just as I looked over at the dining hall, I saw them walking out. I waved to them, and they walked over.

"I see you're headed out already," Nick said, motioning to my suitcase.

"Unfortunately, yes," I said with a sad smile.

"We're just about to head up and pack our stuff," Adam stated.

"I just realized we never asked; where specifically do you live in California, Kinsley?" Justin asked.

"Burbank. What about you guys?" I watched as one by one, smiles spread across their faces—whether from my answer or question, I wasn't sure.

"We live in Pasadena. Maybe sometime we can meet up!" Tommy said with excitement.

"That would be awesome." I summoned my courage and asked something I had been debating whether I should ask for most of the trip. "Do you guys want to exchange numbers, so we can stay in touch?" They all jumped at the chance.

I quickly punched my number in their phones, and they all put theirs in mine. After we finished exchanging numbers, Nick startled.

"Hey guys, we need to go finish packing, or we'll miss our flight," he said.

"Oh yeah, you're right," Adam agreed.

"It was nice meeting you guys. I enjoyed hanging out with this week," I said, smiling.

"You too," "Same here," and "Back at you," were heard from Adam, Nick, and Tommy.

They all started to walk away, only to realize that Justin was still standing in front of me.

"You coming?" Nick asked with raised eyebrows.

Justin hesitated. "Um…" Justin looked from Nick back to me "I'll be there in a minute."

The guys all nodded tand left. I stood there a minute not knowing why he had stayed longer and wasn't saying anything.

Before it got awkward, I decided I needed to see if my parents were ready to leave yet. "Well, I should probably go t—"

Justin cut me off before I could finish. "I know," was all he said.

"You know what?" I asked, furrowing my eyebrows in confusion.

Justin's eyes were locked on mine when he said, "I know about Incognito."

"What about Incognito?" I inquired, slowly pacing my words to emphasize my confusion.

I have no idea what he knows. I'm worried he figured out my secret.

Justin answered, keeping his eyes locked on mine. "I know you are her." There was no hint of doubt in his voice. No flash of disbelief in his eyes.

My eyes widened, and my entire body went rigid. I was caught off-guard by his conclusion. I could barely respond.

"What?" was all I could manage to say. My hands instinctively intertwined.

Justin talked a little more slowly this time, seeming both to put emphasis on carefully chosen words and to give me time to register what he was saying. "I know you're Incognito. You and Incognito are the same person." He said it in a way that made it sound more like a random fact and less like a big secret I'd managed to keep from my parents.

I was shocked he had figured it out, but I still had to try to throw him off. *I'm not ready for anyone to know who I am. He can't know. What's he gonna think of me if I confirm his suspicion? He'll never trust me.*

"You—you're crazy. I'm not her," were the only words I could say. I mentally scolded myself: *come on, Kinsley, you can do better than that. Why am I lying? It's wrong, and he already knows there's no point in hiding. What if he tells the others? What if I can convince him I'm not her?* The conversation was not going well.

"I know you are. I don't understand why you deny it."

I didn't know why, but I continued to challenge him. My inner panic tried to convince me I could change his mind, break the confidence he felt. "Okay, and what exactly makes you think I'm her?" I asked skeptically.

He stood there a moment with a slight smile playing on his lips. "Well, quite a few things. To begin with, both of your voices are the same. You have the same hair color, and you both have the same color of eyes. You have green eyes—"

Before Justin could continue, I argued against his point. "Same color eyes means nothing; lots of people have the same color eyes."

Justin stared at me in disbelief. "Do you know how rare your pure, bright-green eyes are? When I saw you at the masquerade with your mask on, I was only able to see your eyes. That's when I knew for sure that her eyes were exactly the same. That meant you were her; and as if that wasn't enough, when I danced with you at the masquerade, I noticed you both had the same style. When I danced with you, it felt just like dancing with Incognito. You two were one and the same. You both even acted similarly and said some of the same things. You even carried the same bag. And by the way, I believe this belongs to you..." As he said the last part, he reached into his pocket and pulled out something. When Justin opened his hand, there was my beloved bracelet, shining in his palm.

"What? How? Where did you find it?" I asked him. I was more interested in the fact that he'd found my bracelet than that he knew my secret.

"It was in the room you—Incognito—always practiced in," he explained.

"I can't believe I didn't look there," I said in amazement.

When I realized what I had just said, it was too late to take it back. Amidst my shock and joy, I had incriminated myself and confirmed what he already knew.

Justin smiled. "By saying you should have looked there, you just proved that you are Incognito. And you didn't find it, because one of the first times I ran into Incognito, I picked it up. I meant to return it to you immediately, but you were gone by the time I went into the hall to find you. I kept meaning to give it to you, but I never had it with me. I decided to start carrying it in my pocket so I could give it back. The bracelet also helped me fill in the gaps."

"How did my bracelet help you figure out who I was? Why didn't you think it was just solely Incognito's?" I asked, giving up trying to persuade him that I wasn't Incognito. He clearly had figured out my secret; there was no way I could deny it anymore.

"The plane ride. When I took my seat, before I got your attention, I noticed the bracelet you had your sights locked on. The phrase, 'A Princess Never Forgets Her Worth' is kind of hard to forget. I picked up the bracelet and realized Incognito was wearing the same one with the same thing engraved on it."

He knew. He knew everything. He was the only person who knew my secret.

"I figured it all out, but I still don't get one thing," he said.

"What don't you get?" I questioned, still half in a daze.

"Why?" he asked.

What is it with him and these one-word questions? He needs to explain more; he can't just throw out a one-word question and expect me to read his mind and know what he's asking.

I was forced to ask, "Why what?"

Justin elaborated on his question,"Why wear the mask? Why not just do your YouTube videos as yourself? Why all the secrecy?"

It took me a moment to answer, not because I didn't know why. I had been asking myself that question a lot. I knew why. Now I had to find the best way to say it.

"Well, there are a few reasons. First, with the mask, others can focus more on the movement of the dance and not on my appearance. I wanted anyone who watched the videos to pay attention to the dancing and the story I was telling—not who I was or my face. I also didn't want attention. I didn't want to be walking around and have people notice me, if I were ever to get that popular." I paused to let him take in my words.

I continued talking, never breaking eye contact with Justin. "I was doing what others do on a normal basis. I just wasn't hiding the fact that I was wearing a mask. In my mind, it was the same act as everyone else, since everyone pretends to be someone they're not. Everyone hides who they are and acts a certain way for others to see; what I was doing wasn't any different. One could say I was making a statement, but the more I think about it now, I realized I mainly wore the mask out of fear."

I tore my eyes from Justin's gaze and looked at the floor. I was unable to look him in the eye. I mustered what little bit of courage that remained and continued. "I was afraid that when I started to post my videos, I would experience hatred. People would hate my dancing, and they would say I was awful or that I wasn't very pretty. I felt that with the mask, people wouldn't know who the terrible dancer was or what she looked like. I could conceal my identity and hide from hurtful comments. If people didn't know the real me, the comments wouldn't matter as much."

Justin was silent. I scanned his face, trying to read him, but I couldn't tell what he was thinking.

Suddenly he blurted, "Does it work?"

"Does what work?" I asked, not sure what precisely he was asking.

"Hiding behind your mask, so comments don't bother you. Does it work?"

I was silent. I didn't want to answer that question. *The answer is no.*

Justin continued, "You can't just hide who you are in hopes that the comments won't mean anything. As long as you care about what people think, the comments will hurt." He paused, keeping his eyes locked with mine.

I couldn't look away; it was as if a magnet was forcing me to keep eye contact.

He continued, "If you keep your mask on for too long, pretending to be someone you're not, eventually no one will remain under the mask. You won't know who you are. Believe me, I speak from experience."

I considered what he was saying. Justin suddenly added more, "And you're wrong. Not everyone wears a mask."

I was already overwhelmed by what he'd said; I didn't have time to process his last statement.

"What do you mean?" I asked.

"You're right that most people hide their true selves to fit in. I even used to, but not everyone does. The boys and I, the people you've seen this week, that's who we are—no matter who we're around and what we're doing. We have to deal with negative comments from people, but we don't let them affect us, because we don't define ourselves by what other people say about us. Other people don't determine who we are or what we think of ourselves. We only care that we're true to who we are."

Just then my dad called for me from the lobby door. I turned around, held up one finger, and mouthed "one more minute."

I thought about everything Justin had said. When he mentioned the boys, an instant panic rushed into my mind and sucked all the air from my lungs. "Are you gonna tell people my secret—the rest of the guys?" My voice was laced with fear.

"That all depends on whether you are OK with me telling people or not. Do you want me to tell people?" he asked with an even tone.

"No, not yet. I'm not ready for other people to know. My parents don't even know," I said, shifting my gaze to the ground.

A moment passed before he spoke. "Then no one else will know. It will just be our secret."

I smiled at him. "Thank you," I said sincerely, as I raised my head to look him in the eyes.

"However, I suggest if you plan to keep this up for a while, you should tell your parents."

I nodded my head, knowing he was right. "Yeah, I know."

I heard my dad call my name for a second time from the lobby door.

"It was nice getting to know you guys this week," I said, hesitating before I continued. "Justin, who you guys got to know this week, that's the real me. I wasn't pretending to be someone I'm not."

"I know, it was nice to get to know you—*the real you*. I'll stay in touch," Justin said with one final smile.

Justin turned around and began walking toward the elevator, but before he could get more than a few steps away, I said, "That just makes you braver than everyone else."

Justin turned around with confusion written all over his face. "What does?" he asked.

"The fact that you are brave enough to remove your mask." Justin's smile grew. He gave me a nod and then turned to leave.

As I watched him walk away, I knew there was only one question that mattered: *am I brave enough?*

Acknowledgments

This book tested me and shaped me in ways I could never imagine. It taught me that it's a good thing to reach out and ask for help. This book would not have become a reality without these people (and many others).

BREATH OF LIFE:

- God opened my eyes and implanted this idea in my head. Only through Him was this story brought to life.

THE MENTOR:

- Kary Oberbrunner—The one who helped guide me into making my dream a reality. If not for Kary and AAE, I would still be lost, wondering how in the world I was supposed to make a book a reality.

THE CULTIVATOR:

- Alicia O'Roark—Who when I was just a child cultivated my love of reading and writing. If not for your idea to bring in writing teachers to the homeschool program, I would have never discovered my passion for writing.

THE ORIGINATOR

- Kim Meyers and The Arts—The inspiration to have my story take place at a showcase for the arts. Without you, my book would have turned out entirely differently.

THE NEW PERSPECTIVE:

- Cindy Henderson and Samantha Stoner—The first two I entrusted my manuscript to in order to give me another set of opinions and a fresh set of eyes.

- Jocelyn Godfrey Carbonara—The one who fine-tuned my manuscript and helped me keep the intent and story flowing.

THE ARTISTS:

- Lisa Emanuel—The artist who not only designed a killer website but cheered me on throughout this entire process.

- Chris Tobias—The one who made my book come to life with an extraordinary cover.

THE THREE JOVIAL MUSKETEERS:

- Drew Baker, Devin Baker, and Luke Emanuel—The three who bring encouragement and laughter into my everyday life. The three who get me out of my head and encourage me to live life and have adventures. You helped keep the light in this project.

THE IDEA BOUNCERS, THE CHEERLEADERS, AND EVERYTHING IN-BETWEEN:

- Velvet Baker and David Baker—The two who let me continuously bounce ideas off them. The two who encouraged me when I needed it most. The two who wouldn't let me give up. The two who always told me the truth no matter what. These two were at the heart of the project. I never could have made it through this book without their love and support.

Inspirations

These people are the inspirations behind my daily life. These people encourage me, give me something to chase after, and keep me headed in the right direction.

BOOK INSPIRATIONS:

- Kathleen Cooke—A fellow author whose book brought me encouragement for each day. A strong woman who is a culture changer and woman of God.

- Sheri Rose Shepherd—Where my journey to discover my identity all began. Her book, *His Princess: Love Letters from Your King,* was what first made me wrestle with this idea of identity. I am forever grateful for her book that helped me take my first steps toward finding my true identity.

SOCIAL MEDIA INSPIRATIONS:

- Lauren Green McAfee—Her social media presence is a beacon of light. She is a strong woman of God and someone I look up to.

- Promise Tangeman—I get constant encouragement and inspiration from her social media. An entrepreneur who is all about empowering other women.

MUSICAL INSPIRATIONS:

- Colton Dixon, Britt Nicole, For King and Country, and Hollyn—Music is a big part of my life, and these four main artists are my uplifters. These artists have provided me with clarity on my identity and an uplifted spirit.

I wrote these Behind the Mask thoughts to correlate with themes in the book, and I hope they inspire you as you read and reflect on them.

Behind the Mask: Section 1
What Power Does a Mask Hold?

Is a mask a powerful thing?

Does one conceal oneself out of cowardliness?

For what does a mask bring?

Masks often bring weakness

We never show who we truly are

We remain hidden so others won't know,

All the things we have done this far

Ever heard the saying you reap what you sow

Won't you get but another person in a mask

For you don't want people to get close to you

So we continue on our daily task

As if our mask is true

Is anyone brave enough to take theirs off?

No, are you?

Behind the Mask: Section 2
The Lies We Believe

We don't speak the truth. It is human nature to protect oneself. We fear being vulnerable. Sharing truth, especially with the people we are closest to, exposes us to potential harm and pain. It feels a lot safer to keep the truth hidden. *People won't like me once they know the truth*—that's the lie we tell ourselves.

We convince ourselves that for people to like us, we must keep the truth hidden. We bury it. We pile on what we believe people want to see and hear. It's only so long before we start to lose sight of what's real and what's fake. We will come to a point where we can't tell where the lies end and where we begin.

Behind the Mask: Section 3
A Painful Comfort

I suffocate under my mask, yet I do not dare remove it.

My mask has become a sort of safety. My mask protects me from others by not allowing anyone to get close.

I gasp for air and struggle to breathe, yet I leave my mask intact.

As painful as it is not to be able to breathe, I seem to convince myself to remove it would be worse.

I do not want others to see how broken I am. I fear once they know the real me they'll think the same thing I do—*underneath it all, I'm a freak, a monster, a nobody.*

Here I stand suffocating in a prison of my own making.

Behind the Mask: Section 4
Are You Brave Enough?

We all have one. We try so hard to hide our real selves so no one else will see. We cover up our blemishes, but they will never go away. Yet we try to hide them anyway. We don't want people to know we are hiding anything. We act as though *this is my true self.*

We try so hard to conceal ourselves behind a mask so no one can get close enough to see our flaws.

We need to breathe sometimes so we remove our masks in the only time we feel safe—when we are alone, and no one can see our flaws. What we don't know is that there is someone who sees us for who we are. He sees past the mask straight to our hearts. He sees us in the silence by ourselves. He sees the broken people we are—and he accepts us, fake masks and all.

However, He wants so much more for us. He wants us to bravely and proudly remove our masks and say this is who God created me to be.

Sure, you're going to get strange looks, because you're the only one brave enough to show up to a masquerade without a mask. Who knows? You may start a trend and others will begin removing their own masks. When we remove our masks, something beautiful happens. We discover who God truly made us to be. He shows us off to the world and says look at my masterpiece.

I ask, are you willing to remove your mask? You'll be surprised how different you'll feel and how much your view of the world will change. Are you brave enough?

Isaiah 64:8
"But now, O Lord, you are our Father; we are the clay, and you are our potter; we are all the work of your hand."

About the Author

Through her writing and speaking, Toria Leigh (TL) shares her passion for helping people remove their "masks," encourages them to stay true to their own identities, and to begin living fuller lives as their true and honest selves.

In a world where society labels and persuades a person to be something he or she is not, TL struggled with removing her own "mask." She had to wrestle with insecurities and learn what it truly meant to own every side of her identity.

She now invests her time in helping others learn that they are enough. TL helps them become confident in who they are—and who they were designed to be—because she knows that when people remove their "masks" and start living true to their identity, incredible things happen.

Talk with Toria

Toria would love to hear from you. Reach out to her on Twitter, Instagram, or Youtube.

You can even get in touch through her website.

Don't miss
Toria Talk Tuesdays
found on Youtube

Toriah Leigh

or any
of her social media accounts.

@realtorialeigh

torialeigh.com

Bring Toria to Your Youth Event.

Imagine author Toria Leigh sharing about her struggles with identity and how she was able to remove her mask.

--- ★ ---

Toria understands the importance of choosing the correct speaker. The right one can encourage and clarify, but the wrong one could only farther deject and confuse. Her authenticity, willingness to share on her struggles and uplifting content makes her the top choice for many youth events. She tailors her speeches to achieve her client's goal.

Your youth will walk away knowing they are enough.

Contact Toria today to begin a conversation

torialeigh.com